A GREAT STORM RISING

MARTY KINGSBURY

ARCHWAY
PUBLISHING

Archway Publishing books may be ordered through booksellers or by contacting:

Archway Publishing
1663 Liberty Drive
Bloomington, IN 47403
www.archwaypublishing.com
844-669-3957

ISBN: 978-1-6657-2243-8 (sc)
ISBN: 978-1-6657-2242-1 (e)

Library of Congress Control Number: 2022907559

Print information available on the last page.

Archway Publishing rev. date: 05/25/2022

I am a fool
To weep at what I am glad of.
—*The Tempest*, Miranda, act 3, scene 1

The people who need mercy the most
Are the ones who deserve it the least.
—*Shakespeare Behind Bars*

PROLOGUE

"Have you always known?"

"That I'm a lesbian? Yeah. Pretty much. Well, I really figured it out when I was twelve and kissed a boy at summer camp."

Evvy takes my hand, but then she doesn't. She hands me a paddle, and we are in a canoe with a yellow sail and a pink tiller. She's guiding the boat, and we've caught the wind in the middle of the river. The river carries us where we want to go. The sky is as blue as a dream.

Until a storm rises up. Like a cornered tiger, it roars and swallows our little boat, and we're clinging to the sides, and cold water is splashing, filling the boat, and all around me, everything is sinking.

And I am swimming, looking for the surface, but everywhere I swim, I sink deeper into the water. *Evvy!* I'm paralyzed. I turn my head and look for her. I want more than I have ever wanted anything in my whole life to say yes to her, to tell her I love her, to mean every inch of it, and to promise I won't hurt her with my endless lies and swirling confusion.

But then, wow! Look! It's my dog, Arpeggio! Swimming to me. *Hi, Arpeggio!* My words bubble up. Sea turtles float by, yellow ones with pink tails, lumbering in their hefty shells but so graceful. *Evvy, look!* And I point. And then it's dolphins—green with white bellies. They float upward, out of the water, and I follow them, breaking through the surface of the water, gasping for air.

CHAPTER 1

TIME TO GET UP

"Adrian?" I knock on my brother's door, last night's dream a wet, hazy memory. "Time to get up. Monday morning, and we have another week of school."

The house is totally quiet. The only sound is Arpeggio padding down the wooden stairs, his dog nails tapping away.

"You need a manicure." Arpeggio looks up at me and wags his stumpy little tail. "Would you like that? A nice mani-pedi?"

I knock again. "Come on, Adrian. I'm too tired for games this morning. Get up."

But still it is quiet.

I pry the door open. Just a squeeze. The lights are off, but the morning sun wriggles through the curtains and rests on his floor. His pajamas are neatly folded at the foot of his bed. I open the door some more. "Adrian?" My voice bounces off the wall of the empty room. He's not here.

"That's odd," I say to no one. I close the door and tiptoe down the stairs. I don't know why I need to be so quiet, but in a quiet house, a quiet footfall seems right.

"Dad? Mom? Is anyone home?"

My words bounce off these walls too.

"This is really weird." I turn on the lights in the kitchen. It smells of cookies, but there are no cookies on the counter. No dishes in the sink. Arpeggio sits tall by the door, brushing his stubby tail across the dusty floor. But other than that, nothing. No one. I touch the oven. Maybe it's warm from baking. Or maybe it's warm from the heat in the kitchen. I can't tell. The curtains are still closed.

"I've read stories, you know, where one morning you wake up and you're the only person alive on the whole planet, and you have to figure out how to live now that, like, everyone has disappeared."

I turn on the light to the basement. It flickers and then comes on. I creep down the stairs and open the door to the garage. Both cars are gone. I don't know if that's good news or not. I climb the stairs again. The light flickers again when I turn it off.

"Where are they?"

But there on the kitchen counter by the stove, under the World's Best Dad coffee cup that I gave my dad like ten years ago when he *was* still a good dad, is a flimsy slip of paper. Just a corner. A pencil rests in the cup. It's a note. And Dad's near illegible handwriting:

No need to worry. Mom's gone to work. I took Adrian to school. Love, Dad.

"Well, I'll be damned." I laugh, and my heart starts to beat again. "Look, Arpeggio. Dad took Adrian to school! OK then. We are off morning patrol. Do you want to take a walk?"

Arpeggio wags his tail again, running to the door and turning circles. Arpeggio is a three-year-old cocker spaniel, all black with a thin white tuxedo stripe, which starts at his chin and disappears into his belly. He has a stout tail and ears that hang down to his elbows. His joy is infectious. I grab my jacket and his leash from the hooks in the hallway and open the door. "Voila, my puppy." And out he runs.

The morning is cool and clear. It's 6:35 a.m. We set the clocks back this weekend, so, for a few brief days, we are up in the morning light. The sun peeks over the horizon. Pink and lavender ribbons wrap around the trees. The sky is going to be that deep, crystal, azure blue that makes everything sharp. Clear edges. Clean lines. We skip down the rickety stone steps, and the soft yellow leaves of autumn maple trees rustle in the breeze. Today I am even up before Evvy, my sweet girlfriend—the word still flutters in my stomach -- texts in for the morning wardrobe report. No messages. It doesn't matter. Dad is off with Adrian. Mom is off to work. And I am as free as a dog at play. I don't have to get my little brother dressed and fed. I don't have to lead him down these treacherous steps and help him onto the bus. I don't have to talk to my dad, who is usually, by this time, up making some gargantuan breakfast that I can't eat. And I don't have to answer to my mom's ten thousand demands.

Arpeggio stops at all his usual spots, inhaling the roots of trees, the leaves of shrubbery, and the blades of grass. Something snaps behind me, like a twig breaking. I turn, but no one is there. Just my shadow. A blue jay calls from a nearby tree. A chipmunk chirrs and darts across the street. I wave to the horses that are just emerging from the barn for another day out in the field, munching grass. They look at me, blink their big, watery eyes, and lumber into the thin morning sun.

This is pretty amazing. A morning where I don't have to take care of everyone in this stupid house. A morning where I can walk my dog like a regular person, make a little breakfast, get dressed in peace.

"What are you wearing?" That's Evvy texting in. Right on time.

"The same sweats I wore to bed. And you?"

"Very funny. Bus stop in thirty minutes."

And, except for a tiny creepy feeling that lingers in the back of my head, I am officially awoken from my mini-infinity of a morning with no responsibility.

CHAPTER 2

FAREWELL TO THE FALCON

First period is English. Evvy and I were supposed to be in the class together this year. We even had a little bit of time with me here by the windows and her right beside me, and we could pass each other notes, which, of course, I did, but she never did 'cause she's such a good student. But then, last week, they up and transferred her to art. They said they want her to work with the freshmen on some something or other. I really should listen to her better. And she was super excited about it. I remember that much anyway. But when she told me she had to change her schedule, I kind of glazed over. I was so sure they knew, that everyone knew, that she kissed me, I mean, really kissed me, and I really, really kissed her back, and that was why they moved her out. But she said it wasn't that at all, that this was a chance, a real chance to do her art, and she'd see me at lunch. That's wonderful for her, but once again, I'm in here on my own.

This is the first time in I don't know how many years that I've come back to the same school for a second year. Dad goes crazy. Dad loses his job. Dad finds a job somewhere else. We move. That's been my MO since I was six. I still don't know a lot of these kids, but at least they look familiar. Less snobby than they looked last November when I arrived on the scene in black leggings, Doc Martens, and a baggy sweater. I thought I was the coolest thing on the planet till I discovered that the really cool girls, except Evvy of course, wear pretty little skirts and nice shoes, their hair brushed fifty times so it shines in the morning sun. Evvy is also impeccably dressed: she always looks dashing in her linen trousers with a button-down shirt and vest. Or sometimes suspenders. Or sometimes a loose tie. I liked her right away. That wasn't what surprised me. What truly surprised me was the fact that she liked me too.

Anyway, it's the beginning of October, and I'm back in my old seat, third desk in the row by the windows. I like this seat. I can watch the seasons change.

I take a breath and remind myself that I don't have to be afraid. I lean across the aisle where a girl who goes by the name of Tiger sits. Mr. Harrison called her Sandra once, but she set him straight on that in a New York minute. She dyed her hair orange and black, hangs seven earrings off her left ear, and wears more makeup and tighter clothes than Dolly Parton. "Did you do the homework?" I ask.

She shakes her head and snaps her gum. "My boyfriend came over. I haven't seen him in a whole month cause he's at UMass." She doesn't look at me. "Did you?"

"I started to. I fell asleep on it, though, and I had the most amazing dream. I was swimming with these pink and yellow dolphins and sea turtles and—"

"Oh." Now she looks at me.

"And there was this magical island, and the birds all declared me to be their queen, and they showered me with rose petals." I lie. I know I do, but she's looking at me, and I think she wants to smile, so I keep talking. I want her to know that under all my layers of black clothes, I am super interesting too. I smile my best we-could-be-friends smile.

She snaps her gum. "We watched a movie. And made out."

Mr. Harrison opens the door and sings, "Good morning, everyone." He balances a big pile of books under his chin, and somehow he manages to walk in and close the door with his foot. "I trust you slept well this weekend and wrote your final paper on WB Yeats. Yes?"

The books spill onto the desk, and he straightens them out. A little. Kim, a new girl who sits in the second row by the door, and who it seems is vying for the spot of Mr. Harrison's pet, leaps to her feet to help. But Mr. Harrison puts his hand up, and she stops, slinking back into her seat. She's in pigtails and a pretty little blue jumper with a yellow T-shirt. Is she really a cool kid, or like the rest of us, is she just desperate to look cool? She smiles at him. It's disgusting. Does she even know he's gay?

Mr. Harrison stands there for what seems like half the period, staring at the pile of books. Except for the squeaking of a few chairs, no one makes a sound. And then he turns around.

"Yes. All righty then. Before we step gingerly back into the world of Shakespeare—"

We moan. Of course we moan. I mean, do we have to drag ourselves through the language of Shakespeare? Again?

"Oh stop. What did you think was going to happen? Tiddlywinks by the fire? This is English, my friends. The great works! But before we set out on our journey, do you have any last questions about Mr. Yeats? Irish Nobel Laureate of 1923?" No one does. "Founder of the Abbey

Theatre in Dublin?" We are as quiet as stones in a sleepy river. We know if we ask anything, it will be another half hour diatribe on "the widening gyre." The separation of civilization and nature. Alienation and deterioration. Again. We've heard it seven times already, but Mr. Harrison sweeps his arm across the room and recites it for the eighth time anyway:

Turning and turning in the widening gyre
The falcon cannot hear the falconer;
Things fall apart; the center cannot hold;
Mere anarchy is loosed upon the world—

And once again, I don't know how he does it, because even though he has recited these lines a gazillion times, I am lost in the music of his voice. The bird in the sky, its wings spread across the clouds, flies out of reach with no thought to the consequences of freedom. Does it want to hear its person, or is this its chance to escape, to once again be a bird of the wild?

"All righty then. Let us keep anarchy in our memory and this marvelous bird in our hearts now and forevermore as we turn our attention back to the theater, to the magic of lights and costumes and mystical worlds. I usually do this play with my juniors, but since this is your last year in high school—"

"No," we say. "We are juniors."

"Juniors? Really? But you look so mature!"

Yeah. We laugh. We relax. Even in the daunting shadow of William Shakespeare with his thees and thous and flipped around sentences, we know we are ready. Mr. Harrison smiles at us—it's all he has to do, a simple twist of the lips—and we settle into his world.

He places his palm on the stack of Shakespeare. "Okey dokey then. Our Shakespeare play this year will be his last play, *The Tempest*." He strides up and down the aisles, passing out books—sacred books, each and every one, new, old, crisp, or dusty. It doesn't matter. They are books. Road maps for what lies ahead. So many juniors have traveled these pages before us, and now it is our turn to take this journey, to ride the waves of Shakespeare.

"*The Tempest*," he says, "is neither comedy nor tragedy, though it has elements of both. *The Tempest* is, in fact, one of Shakespeare's two romances. *Winter's Tale* is the other one." He looks around the room, making eye contact with each one of us. He grins. "Yes. I knew you were all dying to know that little tidbit of information. Yes, indeed, *The Tempest* is a play about magic: what lies in the natural world and what lies just below, in the supernatural world. It is about the horrors that come with colonization, when one people has the privilege and the audacity to own another people. And it is a play about revenge and power. At least that is how it begins. In the end, it is a play about acceptance, forgiveness, about giving everything up and granting the greatest wish of all: freedom."

He goes to the board and writes *Forgiveness* in great big letters. There is a shuffling of paper as we open our notebooks and write *Forgiveness*, also in big letters.

"Everyone ready? Let us begin at the beginning where, true to Shakespeare, there is a terrible storm at sea. A tempest." He opens his book, but then he stops and looks at us. "Are you all aware that the school play this fall will be *The Tempest*? Yes, indeed. I've wanted to do this play for many years now, and I finally have the go-ahead. Auditions will be held a week from this Friday. After school. I hope many of you will consider trying out. There are some wonderful roles in this play."

This time, when he looks around the room, I swear, for an instant, his eyes rest on mine. My heart skips a beat.

"But! Let us to the business at hand. Act one. Scene one." He looks at his watch, and then at the door, and then back at us. "*The Tempest* opens on a ship. Alonso, the king of Naples, and his men are returning home from a wedding when suddenly, out of nowhere, on a beautiful day with the wind at their backs, a storm rises from the sea. And it is ferocious." He drums the desk, and thunder echoes off the walls. "Yes! This is one of Shakespeare's favorite ways to open a play. Open with some drama, some sound. Bring everyone off the streets and into the theatre. Catch their attention, so 'Har the mainsail!'"

Mr. Harrison stops and looks around, that quirky smile spreading across his face. We all get very quiet. He wraps the invisible mainsail line around his wrist and walks back to his desk. He holds on tight.

"But this isn't just any storm." The winds pull him. He nearly loses his footing. "Because on board the ship is another king—Antonio, the evil brother, the one who stole the kingdom of Milan out from under the nose of our hero, Prospero. Twelve years ago. And this storm is Prospero's chance for revenge. He's been in exile, hanging out on this island for twelve long years, waiting for this moment to happen—and now, *boom*!"

That wakes us up.

"Oh yes." He holds the mainsail taut. "It's big. A huge storm that will capsize the ship and throw everyone into the sea. 'Boatswain!'" he calls, stumbling back onto the ship, still pulling the invisible line. And when he sways from one foot to another, the whole room seems to wobble, like a mighty ship in the storm.

"Down with the topmast! Yare! Lower, lower! Bring her to try with main course."

Desperately, Mr. Harrison clamors onto his desk, pushing the last few books onto the floor and toppling the invisible sail that has hung over our desks this whole time. Who knew? But down the mainsail comes with a silent clatter, and the kids in the middle rows duck under its gravity.

"Mercy on us! We split, we split. Farewell, my wife and children! Farewell, brother! We split. We split."

And with that, he releases the mainsail line and leaps from his desk, swimming against all odds toward the door, toward dry land. He clamors onto the shore, pulling himself up the wall, a man exhausted from the tides, the current, the sheer, massive power of storm. He stands there, puffing and panting. Kim offers him some water, but he stumbles off, back to his desk, where he stands, taking a deep breath and looking around the room. He is lost, but his feet move, one after the other, toward the sanctuary of his desk. He looks at his watch again.

Something is going on with him.

"On what strange paradise have these characters now landed? The air is sweet and clear. The rocks are dry, and trees still stand, not a branch or a twig out of place."

Mr. Harrison perches on his desk again. His feet dangle. "Now, my friends, gather round. It is time for a little backstory."

We lean in.

"Twelve years ago, twelve long, isolated years ago, Prospero, the would-be king of Milan, and his daughter, the just four years old and innocent Miranda, were tossed out to sea on a ship with no sail. He had his magic books, some clothes, and a little bit of food and fresh water. But honestly, that ship should have sunk. Prospero—remember Antonio? The evil brother? Well, this is Prospero, the 'good' brother." He air quotes *good*. "He and his and his daughter should have both drowned. Maybe it was magic. Maybe it was luck. At any rate, they didn't drown. They came ashore on this tiny island. And for the last twelve years, Prospero has been raising Miranda, just the two of them, a tiny family on this deserted island. He enslaved the two inhabitants of the island: Caliban, an ugly, deformed beast, adorned with fishy scales and the smell of something that's been in the fridge too long. This character lives in the roots and trunk of a tree. And Ariel—sweet, charming Ariel, an airy spirit. Prospero may have studied the magic books, but Ariel is the one who performs his bidding.

"And Prospero has waited. And watched. And waited. Until this very morning, when his brother, Antonio, is at sea, when he calls upon Ariel and all the gods to bring this tempest to his ship! The time of revenge has come! And now the fun begins." Mr. Harrison claps, a snapping sound that echoes off the windows.

"So, let's have some fun, shall we? Let's give Antonio and his men a Magical Island welcome as they come ashore and find themselves not only alive but healthy. And not only healthy but in clothes that are as fresh as the day they put them on. Not clammy or sticky with salt water. Pretty cool. OK? Got it?"

We nod.

"Okey dokey then. For tomorrow, read act one and summarize—in your own words, people! Don't go peeking on Wikipedia— Prospero's history and why …" He pauses. He looks at his watch. He looks at the door. He's thinking. Mr. Harrison never thinks. He never pauses. He's the most confident and together teacher I have. "What happened between these two brothers? That's all."

We gather our books. I am almost out the door when he calls me back.

"Oh, Edwina?"

"Yes, Mr. Harrison?"

He doesn't move, so I close the door and step up to him. "Yes, sir?"

"I would like you to consider auditioning for the role of Ariel."

"Me, sir?"

He grins at me. "Are you surprised?"

I gulp. "Um. I don't know what to say."

"Read the whole play through three times. Get to know this character. Ariel is the fairy sprite, the character who must do Prospero's bidding, no matter how ridiculous the request might seem and no matter how many times Prospero will break his promise to give her the release she has so justly earned. It's a wonderful role, full of opportunity for creativity, and I think you would do well with it."

"Wow. Thank you, sir. I'll ask my mom. I'll ask her tonight. Thank you." And I stand in front of him, waiting for him to say something. Anything.

He looks at his watch, holding the sleeve of his shirt open for the longest time. "That's all," he says.

And I slink out backward. I can't get this stupid grin off my face as I bump into the door and head for the hall.

CHAPTER 3

———⚬⚬⚬———

LUNCH, FINALLY

Mr. Harrison's invitation rings in my ears. In driver's ed, the teacher chatters on and on about seat belts and car accidents and numbers, big numbers with lots of zeros that dance across the board like so many fairy spirits. By the time I get to history, *The Tempest* is burning a hole in my book bag. I stare at the clock as the big hand inches its way toward lunch.

Evvy is at the corner table, her lunch from home spread out in front of her.

"Evvy! Guess what!" I pull my lunch out of my bag: a Pop Tart and some Ritz crackers.

"Where's the feast of thieves your dad makes you for lunch?

"Yeah. My dad. He took Adrian to school this morning, so I was on my own. No seven-course cold lunch today."

"Really? See, Teddy? You do have a normal house. Getting up to drive him to school. That's wonderful."

"Yeah. And Arpeggio and I had some quiet time this morning. It was amazing."

Evvy has three reusable containers with sliced cucumber, sliced apples, crackers, ham, cheese, a bag of potato chips, and a bottle of cranberry juice. She eats slowly.

"Is that your news?"

"What? My dad? No! Get this—Mr. Harrison! He asked me to audition for *The Tempest,* He told me about the role of Ariel and said I should read the play three times and—me! He asked me to audition!"

"Teddy! That's great." She throws her arms around me and gives me a big old hug that fills my body with love and possibility.

"You should audition too. He says there are some really cool roles."

"I'm designing the set and costumes. With the freshmen. Remember? That's why they transferred me to art class."

"Oh, yeah. But what if we could both be in it together? We could run lines and do scenes together. Wouldn't that be just the coolest thing? Ever?"

"Not going to happen. Want some potato chips?"

"They're not barbeque, are they?"

"Wait. Shh." She lifts one ear. "Do you hear that?"

I listen, and mostly all I hear is the incessant din of the cafeteria—trays clattering, books slapping the tables, and kids honking at some terrible jokes. But then, underneath it all, music hangs in the air. It's one note at first, but then three more follow—sweet notes that whisper like the wind in the treetops. And out of the shadows comes Theo, probably the weirdest dude in the whole school. Not creepy; just weird. He's like a mushroom after a rainstorm the way he—poof—shows up. Always the most inopportune time and always, always spinning notes from his harmonica. Sometimes his music is as soothing as cool water. Other times it's haunting and full of shadows. But wherever Theo is, his music is there with him. He pushes his glasses—red this year—up his nose and brushes his black hair off his face with his fingers. His hair is the same as it was last year, just long enough to hang over one eye and his ears, just long enough to shake when he needs to impress someone. His smile is still crooked. Girls fall for him, but then, after two weeks, they run.

"Good morning, ladies."

"Hi, Theo," I say. "How's it hanging?"

"How's it hanging? Really, Carson? You some kind of hip chick now? Damn, girl. Give it up. You'll never be hip and cool."

He gives a quick bow, throws his leg over the back of a chair, and sits with us. He rests his elbows on the table and looks right at me. He smiles, but his eyes are serious. "So, Carson, did you read your horoscope this morning?"

I want to laugh, but there is nothing in his stony expression that indicates humor. "Really? My horoscope?"

"Gemini, right?"

"Yeah." My heart pounds in my chest. My head throbs. "How did you know that?"

"Lucky guess." Now he laughs, an insidious breath of victory. He runs up the scale on his harmonica. "It's not that hard to figure out. You can never make up your mind. And you're always thinking about something else."

"I am?"

"Anyway, it's not good. But since I'm your friend, I thought I should warn you." He takes out his phone and flicks it on. The horoscope is there: *October 10. Gemini. Be prepared for a big surprise today, and not one that you will like.*

"What's that supposed to mean?" I ask.

Theo grins and shrugs.

"You don't really believe this stuff, do you?" Evvy asks.

"Just saying." Theo slides his phone back into his pocket and stands, swinging his leg over the back of the chair. "You don't want my help? Fine. But don't say I didn't warn you." And with that, the music of the treetops disappears into the din of the cafeteria.

I watch him walk away, his harmonica glued to his lips. Other girls watch him, too, stopping their conversations midsentence to listen to his music as he glides through the crowd. His hips sway side to side, and I realize he isn't as tall as he pretends to be. He has heels. Clunky two-inch man-heels but heels nonetheless.

I turn to Evvy. I want to say something about how it was a surprise this morning, a nice surprise, that my dad took Adrian to school, because he never does stuff like that, but now he's doing so much better, and how it was another super surprise when Mr. Harrison asked me to audition, so, "*So there, Theo*," but before I can say anything, she asks, "Did you have English class this morning?"

"I did."

"Was Harrison weird?"

"Weirder than normal, you mean?"

"Exactly. Weirder than normal. Was Harrison weirder than normal?"

"Well, he kept looking at his watch. He never does that. He usually runs right up to the bell."

"Mmm." She leans back and crosses her arms. None of this conversation makes any sense to me because now I am in a fog, and Theo is the foghorn. "Then it is true."

"What's true?" I ask.

"Well," she leans in and whispers. "I heard that he's going to retire. Or at least take a year off. He and his husband are trying to adopt a kid. A baby, I think. They were supposed to find out sometime in the next couple days."

I manage to get, "Wow! How wonderful," out of my mouth. I don't think Evvy has noticed how far away I have drifted in this conversation.

"And," she adds, "I guess Harrison won the coin flip to be the stay-at-home dad." She chatters on, imagining a world where Mr. Harrison is a dad. "But retiring?" she asks. "Leaving? I can't imagine this school without him. He's the heart and soul of poetry." I stare at my food, and it stares back at me. *A dad.*

I drift off to me and Adrian and Dad that day we drove to the lake in Minnesota and went fishing. It was Adrian before he lost his eyesight and Dad when he was World's Best Dad, Dad before he got sick, Dad when he was still fun, and we rented a canoe and paddled out into the middle of the lake and jumped off and swam around the boat and climbed back in, and then it started to rain. A soft, gentle rain, but we were already as wet as wet could be, so it was all good. Sometimes we would just do that. Get lost in the sky, and then we would turn around and find our way back, and we'd be home in time for cocoa, and Mom would have a chicken roasting in the oven, and we'd walk in, and the whole house would smell of family and joy— until the bell rings, and it's time to go to science.

CHAPTER 4

LATE BUS

"Hi, Dad. I'm home."

Arpeggio appears at the top of the stairs. He looks sleepy, but he wags and trots down to greet me with a lick on my hand. There is nothing in the oven. There are no new dishes in the sink. No new note on the counter. I creep upstairs and knock softly on Dad's bedroom door. Still no answer.

"Huh. That's odd. Where's Dad?"

Arpeggio does not answer. I grab his leash, and we head to the bus stop to wait.

"Theo," I tell my dog. "Do you remember Theo?" I run an air harmonica back and forth across my lips, humming like a robin. He looks at me with those watery eyes and thumps his little tail. I believe he understands everything I say. Which seems a little unfair, since I only understand about a tenth of what he is saying. "At lunch today, Theo showed me my horoscope, and it said I was going to get a surprise today. But not one that I would like. Isn't that, like, so weird? I mean, out of the blue, he shows up, tells me this, and then he leaves. Whoosh. In a river of music. I haven't spoken to him since we saw him at the fairgrounds in August. Do you remember that? You liked him. You curled into his knees and—oh, never mind. It doesn't matter. I've made it this far with only good surprises. 'Cause after English class today, Mr. Harrison—"

The bus pulls up, but Adrian doesn't get off. The driver waves and smiles as the door closes and the bus pulls off.

"He's probably on the late bus," I tell Arpeggio. "We'll come back later."

I take out *The Tempest* and settle down at the dining room table to read act 1, scene 2. It's thick and dense—a whole lot of blah-blah about Prospero and his brother and kingdoms and betrayal. I like it when Ariel shows up though. She is a feisty little sprite. Prospero may think that he carries the power of the universe, but really, when it comes down to it, it's Ariel who does all the work. That is so typical of a man.

The afternoon sun sinks low in the sky. I am loving the quiet of the house this afternoon. It's never quiet, except when Dad is depressed, and then no one can move, and the house throbs under the weight of his silence. But today it is quiet because it is at peace, and now that the storm is over and Prospero is just hanging with his daughter, Miranda, on the island, Ariel finds her moment: she is going to beg for her freedom. She has done everything that was asked of her—the storm, the safety of all those men, the safety of the ship—even keeping their clothes clean and pressed through that horrible swim to shore. And now it is her turn.

All hail, great master! Grave sir, hail! I come
To answer thy best pleasure; be't to fly
To swim, to dive into the fire, to ride
On the curled clouds: To thy strong bidding task
Ariel and all his quality.

"*His* quality?" I stare at the page, and read again. "'To thy strong bidding task / Ariel and all *her* quality.' Yes. That's better."

Arpeggio thumps his tail. He likes it when I read aloud to him.

"She has a lot of things she can do, doesn't she? Fly, swim, dive. Yeah. Fire, water, air. She can tackle all the big stuff. You want me to read it again?"

But the room is fading into dark, and it's time to pick up Adrian. "Shall we meet the late bus?"

I grab the leash again and open the door. The sky hangs heavy, like cow udders hungry for milking. The air smells sweet, like snow, but it's only October. Even in the foothills of the Berkshires, that seems a little soon. Arpeggio dances out, and we walk around the corner just as the bus pulls up.

I stand at the door, but the driver shakes his head. "Didn't Jackson tell you? He wasn't in school today."

"Oh, yeah," I lie. "My mom, um, she wanted to know if, if his lunch box was with you."

"Lunch box? Nope. Didn't see it. Sorry."

"Oh, well. It has to be someplace."

The driver closes the door, and the bus rumbles around the corner.

"That's odd," I say. "Where's Adrian?"

Mom is home when we walk back in the door. She's unpacking groceries. "I was wondering where you were. Looks like a storm is coming." I don't say anything, and she looks at me. "Teddy? Are you all right? The house is so quiet."

"Adrian wasn't on the bus," I tell her.

"Really? That's funny. Well, you put this stuff away. I'll call the school." She starts to leave but calls over her shoulder, "I bought that kind of bread you like so much. That organic stuff."

"The driver said he wasn't in school."

"Really?" She comes back into the kitchen. "That is odd. Well, let me call his phone."

Mom punches in the numbers.

Adrian is blind—well, almost blind. He was born with some kind of rare eye disease, and ever since he was six or seven years old, it's all been going downhill. He goes to this special school where they teach him to swim, play a weird kind of basketball, read Braille, and run. And he's a ghost whisperer. Seriously. He knows if someone's spirit is coming or going and if it's happy or sad. And so for his birthday, Mom got him a brand-new Braille phone, which he loves more than life itself. He can text, email, talk—all this stuff that regular kids do. It seems to take forever. The numbers slide off her fingers one at a time.

And on the sideboard, his phone rings.

My stomach sinks.

"Oh my God. Where is your father? Sullivan?" She practically runs to the foot of the stairs and calls again. "Sullivan?"

"He's not home either. There was a note on the counter. This morning. He said he was taking Adrian to school. But nothing this afternoon."

"Oh, Lord. I'll call him. He's bound to know something."

But his phone rings on the sideboard too.

Mom and I stare at each other. Neither of us knows what to say. I pick up their phones. There's one message on Dad's phone. A text from his doctor's office reminding him of his appointment on Monday. Nothing on Adrian's.

The room goes dark.

Mom wraps her arms around me. I lean on her, and she holds me close, rubbing the back of my head. Her blood churns through her veins, and air moves through her lungs. I must be crying because her shoulder is wet. Damp. I think she wants to cry, but I feel her strength.

"We'll find them, Teddy. They have to be somewhere."

"I'll call the police." I sniffle.

CHAPTER 5

THE DETECTIVE ARRIVES

"I'm as good as on my way," the detective tells me. He's sounds so calm on the phone, like nothing would ruffle his feathers. But still, the next ten minutes are the longest ten minutes of my whole life. Mom makes tea for us, and we sit at the kitchen table, and if I didn't know better, I would say this is really normal. But it's not normal, is it? It's 4:45 on an October afternoon, and my dad and my brother aren't home.

Mom peppers me with questions. *When did I find the note? What did I do after school? Why didn't I call her? Where could they be?*

There's nothing I can say except "I don't know, Mom."

"I know. I'm not blaming you, honey. It's just that—well, where are they?"

"I don't know, Mom."

It all seemed so plausible this afternoon. Dad has been doing so much better these days, and it's been such a relief to see him crawling out of that dark hole and being happy again. Whistling. Tapping rhythms with his fingers on every surface. He hears music in every-thing: tables, chairs, bannisters, stairs. The world is his drum set. And he's been talking about his dreams again—maybe going back to work. Hell, just three days ago, he was standing right there, refrigerator door open, cold air spilling out, promising that he would be a better dad for me and Adrian. He said he knew he'd been terrible, that he has some disease, maybe schizophrenia, maybe narcissistic personality disorder, maybe bipolar disorder—the doctors keep changing their minds—so the meds work for a little while, but then they don't, and it's not his fault, but it's kept him so far away from us for so very long. But he's better now. *These latest meds* … He told me that. He promised.

"I don't know, Mom," I say in answer to some question that I do not hear. "Can I go call Evvy?"

"No. Stay with me." She dumps her tea down the sink and paces a path between the dining room windows and the kitchen. She picks up a clean pan and puts it in the sink. She picks up a dirty glass, wrapping her hand around it like a fist. I think she's going to throw it, but she doesn't. She dumps it in the sink. It does not break. "Where are they?"

"I don't know, Mom."

By the time the detective shows up, it's all starting to sink in. He wipes his feet, takes off his coat, and asks, "May I?" He drapes it on a chair. "Detective Malloy, Crystal Falls Police Department." He puts out his hand.

"Harriet Carson." Mom takes his hand, and they shake. He looks her in the eye, and she looks at his shoes. Brown shoes with black pants. Oh my. I see we're working with a fashion faux pas here. "And this is my daughter, Edwina."

"Teddy." I try to smile, but I am locked in with his shoes.

He wastes no time. He flips open a notebook and takes out a stub of a pencil. He licks the lead point, looks at his watch, and writes down the time—4:54. "Now. You said something about your husband? What's his name?"

"Sullivan," Mom tells him.

"Sullivan Carson? From the Native American Museum? I know him. Well, I met him once. A charming man. Absolutely delightful. You say he's missing?"

"Yes," Mom says. "And my son, Adrian."

"How long?"

Mom looks at me. I shrug my shoulders, but I tell the detective about the note on the counter and Adrian's bus driver. He writes that down.

"Did you have any sense that anything was, well, you know, wrong?"

Mom stares at him in disbelief.

"Just asking. Routine questions. Nothing more."

She shakes her head. She seems very far away.

"Sullivan is the legal father, yes?"

"Yes, he is," Mom says.

The detective scratches his neck. "I'm sorry to have to ask you this, but were the two of you in some kind of custody battle?"

"No! Of course not."

"Hmm. I'm not sure what I can do here. As the legal father, he has the right to go someplace with his son." He closes his notebook, but he doesn't put it in his pocket. "Legally, he doesn't need to tell you where he is going. I'm sorry, but my hands are pretty much tied."

"But my son is—"

"Mom. Tell him about the cell phones."

And she does, lurching three steps across the dining room, leading him from the table to the sideboard.

"The phones were here, you say? On the sideboard?" Detective Malloy opens his notebook again.

"Yes," Mom insists. "Right here. Look." And there they still are. Plain as day. Like two rabbits in a warren. "Adrian would never leave without his phone."

He takes a glove out of his pocket and steps up to the sideboard. He looks at the phones first one way and then another. "And this is ..."

"Braille," Mom says. "Yes. My son is blind."

"I see. Yes. Well, that makes things more difficult, doesn't it? Tell me, Mrs. Carson, they've been gone since this morning? Can you be more specific?" he asks. "What time this morning?"

"Well, I left for work at five. Sullivan was up already. He's often up in the night. He was in the kitchen. Right here." And she leads the detective into the kitchen and indicates a spot in front of the oven. "He was whistling and smiling. I remember that. He was making cookies, I think. Yes. Cookies. The kitchen was a terrible mess, and I told him he had to clean it up before I got home. I remember it smelled like sugar. But he was still here. I swear he was."

"I believe you." The detective looks at me over his glasses, his steely gray eyes peering through me.

"I woke up at six fifteen," I say. "They were gone."

"And the kitchen?" he asks.

"It was clean," I tell him. "But I could still smell the cookies."

"Mmm. This morning." He looks at his watch again. "If we estimate the time of departure at six o'clock, that's just eleven hours. That's not very long. We usually wait twenty-four. People show up, you know. It gets dark. They get hungry. They come home." He takes off his glove, closes his notebook, and slides them both into his pocket. "Shame to waste so much police time on something that usually solves itself."

"You mean you're not going to help us?" Mom crumples into a chair at the kitchen table.

"Mmm. Yes. Um." He inches toward the dining room, but then he stops. "Mrs. Carson, is there any place you can think of where he might have gone? Any other family?"

"He had a brother in … I don't know. Anthony Carson. Last I heard, he was in Canada. Sullivan and I lived with him when we were in Las Vegas. That must be, oh, sixteen years ago," Mom tells him. "Sullivan has been mumbling about him in his sleep. But no … it's impossible. They haven't spoken in years."

"Can you call him?" the detective asks.

"I … I'm sorry. I really don't know how."

"Mmm. I see." Detective Malloy tilts his head, detective talk for "Follow me," and I do. He turns on a lamp in the living room and looks around, peering into every shadow and crevice. It all looks stiff and pale: beige carpet, beige wallpaper, a pale green sofa, a coffee table with water stains, and two wing-back chairs: one yellow; the other one pale blue. They're both faded. In the corner, there's a small bookcase and another floor lamp—cast iron. Very old. The way he looks around makes the whole room feel naked.

"Does your dad have any favorite spots?" he asks. "You know, someplace local where he might have gone off to?"

"I don't know. When we were in Minnesota, we used to drive around a lot, you know, just take off and drive around. He likes doing that sort of stuff. Then, when we moved here, he had a job with the museum, and he, I think in part of his job, he spent time in the mountains. Collecting stories from the different tribes. Are they called tribes out here?"

"I think so, yeah." This detective is not like the cops I see on TV. When he smiles, his whole face fills with wrinkles.

"But that only lasted a little while. Still, I think he knows his way around these hills pretty well. But he never mentioned anything. Not to me, anyway."

He writes that down and then pockets his notebook again.

"Is this my fault?" I ask.

That stops him. He looks at me square on. "What? Your dad and brother have gone missing. How could it be your fault?"

I shrug. "I don't know. I should have, you know, when I found the note this morning, I should have, I don't know."

"Called me?" He kneels and takes my shoulders in his strong hands. He looks up in my eyes. "No. Absolutely not. How were you to know?"

Tears form in my eyes. I sniffle them back, but there they are, hot and wet. My cheeks are burning, and I think I want to pee. The detective tells me it's not my fault, but I barely hear him.

And then my mom is in the doorway, clearing her throat, saying, "Please take your hands off my daughter," and I have to say, "It's OK, Mom," before Detective Malloy drops his hands and stands up.

She steps into the room and puts her arm around my shoulders. It feels tense and heavy. She stares at Detective Malloy, and he steps back. "I called the restaurant where Anthony used to work, and they said that, yes, he is back working there. In fact, he's a manager now, but he is away. On business. He won't be back till next Monday. I asked if they knew his cell number, but they said they couldn't tell me that. Gosh, it's been so long. Sixteen years without a word. I don't know what I would have said if he had answered the phone. But to talk to someone who knows him. Makes it seem like yesterday."

"Thank you. We'll see what we can do." The detective nods. He doesn't look at me. He doesn't even look at my mom. His eyes wander over to the windows: the white curtains with pink lilies winding up to the sky, still crisp and new; the lime green blanket I crocheted when I was twelve draped over the edge of the couch; the braided rug from my grandmother. I wonder what he sees when he looks at these things. A loving family with a history of joy and love? Or dust, when even the dust is trying to hide?

"Is there anyone else?" he asks. "Any place where you think he might have gone? The car is gone, yes?"

"Yes. Of course. He was taking Adrian to school." Mom never takes her eyes off of him.

"Do you think that's what happened?"

Mom flinches. I don't see it, but I feel it in her arm. She takes her hand back and wipes it on her skirt. She twists the fabric into knots and then quickly smooths it out. "I … I'd like to think, but, oh, Lord. I really don't know."

"Yes. Of course. Well, let's hope they come home tonight and everything is fine. If not, however, I would like to get a photograph of Adrian. If you don't hear from them by, say, ten tomorrow, I can put it out on an Amber Alert. Just in case. You understand?"

"You mean an Amber Alert? Like he's been *kidnapped*? Oh, my God. I can't believe this," my mom says.

"We'll wait till tomorrow. But yes. It's standard procedure. Someone might have seen them. Our goal is to help them get home. That's all. OK?"

She nods. She fishes in her pocket and takes out a Kleenex. She sniffles and wipes her nose.

"Thank you, Mrs. Carson. Now, a picture?"

"I have one," I say. "A couple weeks old is all."

"Perfect. Thank you." I take out my phone and show him the picture, and he hands me his card. "And I'll call the local hospitals," he says. "See if there might have been an accident of some kind."

"An accident?" My mom moves into the room behind us, her whole body shaking. "Are you saying they're dead?"

"No, no, no. Not a bit. Please, Mrs. Carson. Try to stay calm. We may want to try everything we can. Please. The system has a lot of options in place, so there is no need to panic. Or worry."

"But it's dark. They're out there. Somewhere. You have to find them."

I can't stand it. Not for another second. I excuse myself and go upstairs to find Arpeggio. I sit by the window staring out at the dark night. The sun has left for the day, and the sky is dark and heavy. It's probably setting over Niagara Falls right now. Maybe it will come back tomorrow. Maybe it won't. I don't know anymore. I guess this is my surprise.

CHAPTER 6

THE TEMPEST

That night, the skies explode. Hot lavender knives flash across the sky, followed by a deafening roar. I hide under my covers, and Arpeggio curls in tight around my knees. Mom and I barely talked, except she kept asking me the same questions: *When did I find the note? Didn't I think it was strange?* And then another round of *Where are they? Where can they be? Why didn't you call me?*

At 10:30, as the second round of thunder cracks, I text Evvy. "R U up?"

But nothing comes back.

"Arpeggio. Look! It's snowing!"

Arpeggio lifts his head, and then he lifts it some more, and indeed, flakes are tumbling from the sky.

I slide out of bed and open the curtains wide, filling the room with a glassy light. Arpeggio perches next to me, his front paws on the windowsill, his nose against the glass. I kneel beside him, and the two of us watch, shoulder to shoulder, wriggling in close and then closer, as snow dances in the streetlights. It snows sideways, and then it twirls in circles, and then it snows up. I know it's a slave to the whims of the wind, but watching it like this, the flakes seem to celebrate their space in the cold air.

Shoulder to shoulder, we watch until my knees start to ache. We breathe hot breath on the window, fogging it up and wiping it off, and still it snows. It sticks to the tree branches and fills the grass, and still more snow tumbles from the sky.

"It's magic, isn't it?" Arpeggio tilts his head the way he does so often when he's trying to understand me. "You have no idea what I'm talking about, do you?

"Magic," I explain. "It's something that seems to come out of nowhere."

First snow of the season. I've seen snow a million times: flurries, storms, blizzards, and everything in between. I've seen it in Colorado and Minnesota and Vermont, but wherever I am, the first storm is always a thing of beauty. Trees become goddesses. Familiar streets become unworldly. I am a tiny speck in a vast world.

I crawl back into bed. Arpeggio curls back up at my knees, his breath long and deep. The snow falls behind me, its magic blanketing the world around me.

"If this were a play, I would say Prospero and Ariel were behind this storm."

I lean against the wall. "Because, you know, yesterday it was like beautiful. Fifty-seven degrees. Tonight it's snowing. Mom said it smelled like snow, and she was right. Of course. She always is. But it still feels like it came up out of nowhere." Arpeggio tilts his head. He so wants to understand me. He listens with his whole being. I touch his head and scratch him behind his ear. "Just imagine you're on a ship, way out to sea. It was a beautiful day until suddenly ..."

Arpeggio tosses his chin onto my knee and looks at me, his little tail thumping away. "Drumroll please!" I open *The Tempest* and flip through the pages, looking for Ariel. And there she is, sitting with Ferdinand on the rocks. Ferdinand is Alonso's son, a strapping young prince of sixteen or so. Just about the same age as Miranda, Prospero's daughter. Poor Ferdinand. He looks out to sea, lost and alone. Ariel might be invisible, but her music is everywhere. She takes out her flute, filling the air with magic, and she sings:

> Full fathom five thy father lies
> His bones are coral made

Whoa, wait up here. Hold the phone. I thought everyone lived through the storm. Fresh clothes and all. What's this "full fathom five" stuff? Is Ariel telling this kid that his father drowned in the sea? That nothing is left of his body but bones, and that those are like coral?

I close my eyes, and Adrian is in the car with Dad, off the road somewhere, up in the mountains with snow peleting the car. Lightning flashes, and the hills open up to infinity. Adrian is crying. Dad's trying to comfort him, but he's not very good at it because he's really pissed that Adrian is such a baby. He pushes his hand toward Adrian's shoulder and then pulls it back. They talk about stuff, but I can't really hear it, something about how "it will be OK, Adrian. Just wait and see." How "Come tomorrow, the storm will pass, our clothes will be fresh, and we'll go back home."

When Adrian was seven, he started to lose his vision. He went to see most every doctor in Denver, but none of them could say what was happening. He went through a couple months where it all dropped off really fast, and every morning he woke up terrified even to open his eyes. He was trying so hard to be brave and to live in his new body where he couldn't keep his balance or pour a glass of water or hit the porcelain with his pee, and he didn't know any of the rules of how to get by, and there was this one afternoon when the leaves were turning yellow and the landscape seemed to ripple out forever. I was in the back seat, and he was in the front, and Dad was driving, and I think we were coming back from a doctor's appointment where they still didn't know what was happening, and all of a sudden, Dad pulls off the road and slams on the brakes. I think it was getting late, and maybe the sun was going down, and maybe the cold wind was spinning up the little back road of Colorado, but I remember looking out the window at the pink sky and those yellow trees, and the hills were as tender and beautiful as anything I had ever seen. Dad started talking to Adrian, just talking at first, stuff like "The doctors don't know" and "Do you have any ideas?" but Adrian was really scared, and he just sat there like a big bowl of green Jell-O, staring out the window, pretending like he could see the beautiful foliage, and so then Dad started the car again, but we didn't go anywhere, and he stared out the window and said something like, "Just my luck to have a cripple and a weirdo for kids," and Adrian started to cry, and I was sitting in the back seat, scared myself, saying something like, "Can we go, please?"

And then we were going again, and the silence in the car swelled until it filled every inch, and the fields and pastures and trees and cows—none of it looked pretty anymore.

Was that when Dad went crazy? Was this eye doctor, after all those other eye doctors, the significant event that pushed him over the edge? Gave him too much to deal with? Too many people who needed his compassion?

Where are you, Adrian?

When we got home, Mom said it was "unfortunate" that my dad said those things about us, and then she added, real quick, something about how he couldn't help it. Even so, that was before we knew about his illness, whatever it is. She said we should feel sorry for him, that he was in a lot of pain, and sometimes things, well, sometimes things come out.

We just thought he was mean.

The storm drifts to the east, leaving a gentle wind behind. I lie very quietly with Arpeggio still on my knees, snoring softly.

We'll find you, Adrian. I promise.

I close my eyes, and I'm in a car with Evvy, and we're naked as sea lions, rolling around the back seat. Water rushes in through the windows, and we're swimming the currents as easy as easy can be. Next to me is a pink sea turtle, and over there—"Look, Evvy! A dolphin!" It's the same color as the lightning, and it flashes through the water, lighting up the trail it blazes. Evvy swims close to me, and her body is sleek and clean. She points to a bed of coral and two eyes, still open, peering up at me. *Dad?* I try to say, but it all comes out in bubbles. A final crack of thunder wakes me up with a start.

I sit straight up in bed in the pitch-black night. I am drenched with sweat, and my heart is racing. *Evvy. Where is Evvy?* I grope for my phone, but there is nothing there. No message. No email. No text.

CHAPTER 7

MAYBE IT WAS ALL JUST A DREAM

I crawl out of bed and tiptoe down the hall to Adrian's room. Arpeggio is at my heels. Maybe this has all been a dream. Maybe Adrian will be there, sleepy and rumpled in his bed. I'll open the door and say, "Time to get up, little buddy!" And he'll roll over and say, "Already?"

I squeeze the doorknob and open the door a crack. "Adrian?" I whisper.

He's not there. His bed is still pristine.

I punch in Evvy's numbers.

"Teddy?" She's really groggy.

"Sorry," I say. "Did I wake you?"

"Um, yeah. Didn't you hear? No school. I's a snow day. Hold on. I'm going to sit up." The muffle of her bed covers crackles on the phone. "Did it really snow last night or did I dream it?"

"Yeah. It snowed. About a foot, I think. Can you come over?" Already I'm crying.

"Teddy? Did something happen?"

"Adrian's gone." I sniffle.

I hear her gasping on the other end of the line. "Gone?" And then silence.

"Dad's gone too."

"Well, at least they're probably together. I'm sure they're all right."

"No. We don't know what happened." Tears are tumbling down my cheeks, falling like the snow fell last night but less happy. I squeeze my eyes closed, and I see everything: dad's car on the side of the road, the two of them huddled in the front, the pink sea turtles, the two eyes staring up at me from that "full fathom." I tell her about Detective Malloy, and the cell phones, and the note, and—

"Whoa. Slow down. Is anything missing?"

"I don't know!" She's not listening to me. She's asking the same stupid questions that Mom has been asking, and I'm sick of this. I don't want her to ask them too. I want someone to tell me what's happening. I want her to listen to me. "Can you come over?"

"Of course. Just—give me a few minutes to wake up." There is that silence again. It might only last for two seconds, but it seems like forever. "You know, Teddy, they might have just gotten lost," she says. "Holed themselves up in a motel somewhere. I'll bet they're having breakfast right now. I'll bet they're back as soon as the roads are cleared."

"Yeah. Maybe. Thanks. I'll talk to you later."

"Teddy? Wait." Her voice is faint. I've already hung up the phone.

Mom is up, in the kitchen, washing the same plates she washed last night. I kiss her lightly on the cheek, but she pulls away.

"Good morning. Did you get any sleep?" I ask.

"Not much." She doesn't look at me. She stares into the sink as soap bubbles eddy and flow around the plates. "Detective Malloy called at six something. He's said there's no sign of them at the local hospitals. Nothing at the local motels either. I don't know. I guess that's a good thing, but it sure does leave me without answers. Not that anyone cares about me. Anyway, he's coming over. He wants me to look through their closets so that he can put out an Amber Alert. An Amber Alert! It feels so private, and now the whole town will know that I have a crazy husband and a missing child. Can you imagine?" She stares out the window, and indeed, I can imagine. Shadows of the whole town are standing in our backyard, looking in through the kitchen windows, pity written all over their faces. Pity and condensation. Condensation and pity. Can one even separate those two things? I want to say something, but what? "How about you?" she asks. "Did you get any sleep?"

"A little. I think. Although the storm was wild. Woke me up." I grab a clean glass and open the fridge for some orange juice, not because I'm thirsty but because it's something to do.

She looks old this morning. Her hair hangs around her face in red and gray strings that look more like seaweed than hair. Her bathrobe, once a state-of-the-art pale blue terrycloth robe with a belt that she has not tied, is now as gray and haggard as she is; it droops open, exposing her mismatched pajamas. Her breasts flop over her pudgy belly. She was a beautiful woman at one time, full of life and energy and an ambition to be park ranger in the mountains, to protect everything wild. Now she looks old, and when she walks the trails of the Berkshire Audubon with visitors, she comes home tired. She hangs over the sink, gripping the edge for dear life and shaking her head.

"Two nights ago, it seems like forever now, your dad and I were both awake. It must have been around two thirty in the morning. We were talking, like the old days, you know, when we would pillow talk. Sullivan had these dreams to take us all on a vacation. Rent a cabin in Quebec for a month. Go fishing. Live off the land like pioneers. The way he was talking, gosh, Teddy, we were all family again.

"Then—poof. He's gone. Maybe someone hijacked their car. That happens sometimes, you know. You stop at a red light. Someone gets in, puts a gun to your head, and then—boom—at the green light, you're gone." She rinses a plate and sets it in the drain to dry. "I mean, if they were lost, wouldn't they find someplace to ask directions? And their cell phones? On the sideboard in the dining room like that? Both of them together? It doesn't make sense."

"I know, Mom. It doesn't make sense."

"What do you think happened?"

"I don't know." I stand next to her, leaning back against the wet counter. I touch her hand. "Evvy thinks they got lost and checked into a motel someplace. She thinks they're having breakfast and will be home when the roads are clear." I lean over and brush the hair off her face. Her cheeks are hot, and her eyes are swollen. "It's OK, Mom. We'll find them."

She stares out the window past the imaginary pity party and into the woods behind the house. She drifts into another place, another time. I want to say something, but I don't know what. "You know how your dad likes those places that are so remote."

"Yeah. I know."

She slaps the dishwater, and it hits me in the face. "He's a damn fool. I always knew something like this would happen. Twenty years in this hideous marriage, and now this. Gone. Vanished. Fine! Go if you want! But leave me my son!" She yells at nothing.

"Mom—"

"What? Are you going to defend him now?"

"No, but last night, while I was listening to the storm—maybe it was a dream, but I knew in my heart they're alive. They're out there. Somewhere."

"But we don't know where, do we? And we don't know why. Not really. Was it something I did? Something I said? I keep spinning these last days over and over, and I don't know. He kept talking about a plan. A big plan. I didn't pay any attention. I'm so sick of his big ideas that get us into trouble." She sits at the table and hangs her head, staring into the pile of clothes. They were so ordinary yesterday—another pile of clothes needing to be sorted and folded and put away neatly into our drawers. A simple act of love that suddenly feels tender and lonely and overwhelming. Now they're evidence. What was taken? What was left behind? She chokes back her tears. "He's taken off before, I know that, and maybe this isn't any different, but he's always found his way home. And the storm last night. Did you hear that?"

"I did. Yeah."

"Oh, God. Where are they?"

I so don't know what to say to her. I thought I could help. Talk to her. Something. But I don't think there's anything I can say, and I'm afraid that if I say the wrong thing, she'll spin out and turn on me. She's done that before. But this is different. I've never seen her like this, and I want to take her in my arms and hold her, let her cry like she is the child. But I don't. No matter how much I try, I cannot will my arms to leave the wet counter.

"I'm sorry, Mom."

"For what?"

"I don't know. Never mind. I have to get dressed and take Arpeggio out. Come on, puppy."

Arpeggio bounds up the stairs ahead of me. I listen for my mom. I ache to have her call me back, apologize for being so mean, and give me a chance to tell her that I understand that she's scared.

"Teddy?"

"Yes, Mom?"

"No school today, so shovel the walk for me. Please."

"Yes, Mom." And still I listen. And still I hope.

But she doesn't, and once again, so many words go unsaid between us.

CHAPTER 8

THE SNOW HEALS EVERYTHING

I rifle through my clothes, pulling on a pair of leggings, blue jeans, wool socks, and my trusty Doc Martens. I look pretty good, if I do say so myself. Between the snow and my dreams, I didn't get much sleep last night, and the dark circles under my eyes are kind of sexy. Something dark and mysterious about me. I slide this way and that, admiring my sleek body in the mirror. Not skinny. I'll never be cheerleader skinny, but "Look, Arpeggio. I'm getting some shape!"

The dog rolls over.

Has it only been one day? Twenty-six hours since they disappeared? Sixteen hours since we realized they were gone? I know it's not long, but it feels like forever.

"You ready?"

I grab a shovel in the basement, and we step into the foot of snow in the driveway, two feet in the places with drifts. Arpeggio dances and leaps through the snow, but I slog forward, pushing snow as I go. How did I get the impossible task of digging all this snow out? This is Dad's job.

Neighbors emerge from the houses, shovels in hands. "Snow's beautiful, isn't it?" one yells.

"Yeah. That was some freak of a storm!"

"Came up by magic," another yells back.

A snowplow churns by, pushing another small mountain to the foot of the driveway, and I get why Mr. Harrison wants me to audition for Ariel: I am the fairy sprite who is summoned to perform the impossible, the one who must serve the master, no matter how ridiculous it might seem. I wonder if I will ever gain my freedom.

But then suddenly, there is Evvy, an apparition of light and promise, tromping through the drifts with a shovel.

"Hey!" I say. "You came!"

She steps over the small mountain at the foot of the drive and shuffles through the snow. "If you hadn't hung up on me, you would have known I was coming." She looks over her shoulder, first left, then right. Then she kisses me. A light touch on my lips that shivers all the way to the place where the sun don't shine. "Some things are too hard to do by ourselves. And moving all this snow? All by yourself? That is one of those things." She pushes her shovel into the snow and throws it up into the backyard.

I fill my shovel and follow her. "I'm glad you came. I really am. I didn't think …"

She puts her mitten to my lips. "What is it going to take for you to trust me?"

"Probably a miracle, I'm afraid." I dig. I carry. I hurl the snow, but it tumbles back into the driveway. "I think you were in my dream last night," I tell her. "Or maybe two nights ago. I've lost track. We were in a canoe, and then we were swimming. We might have seen dolphins, or maybe we were dolphins, but we were in the river. Then I woke up." I can't look at her. I'll want to kiss her again and again and again, cry big tears into her shoulder, rage at the gods, and I can't do that. I have to be strong for Mom. And for Adrian. I stare at the driveway. One foot deep by ten feet long by what? Maybe eight feet wide? I sniffle back my tears. "I never noticed how big this driveway is. Isn't that funny?"

"You have some fine imagination," she says. And then, from the real world, she adds, "Your dad hasn't come home after a nice hearty breakfast at some motel, did he?" she asks.

"No, he didn't."

"How are you holding up?"

"I don't know. I thought I was doing OK, but my mom … I should have known when I saw that note. Dad never drives Adrian to school. He never does anything to take care of us. Not anymore. I mean, he used to. He used to be a wonderful dad. But that was before. If only I had called the detective then. Told him about the note."

Evvy puts her arm around my shoulder. Her fingers lift up into my hair, and she twirls the ends. Her fingers are cold, but her touch is warm. She doesn't say anything.

"Not that I know what he might have done," I add. "He wears brown shoes with black pants, so that tells you all you need to know about him."

Arpeggio leaps through the snow drifts. His long ears drag behind him. He looks like a dancer. I don't know why I never noticed this. It's funny what you notice and when.

"I was trying to talk to the detective, you know, tell him what I knew. He told me this wasn't my fault, but I was in charge. I'm the one who helps Adrian get on and off the bus. I'm the one who's supposed to come home after school and make supper. My mom is working now. Like all the time. So it's my job to make sure Adrian is OK, and he's not! I don't know where he is!"

She squeezes my waist and whispers in the softest, most gentle whisper imaginable, "Detective Malloy is right. Whatever happened. Wherever they are, it is not your fault."

"I wish I believed that." I surrender. I bury my face in her, lean into her strength, and I cry. I cry great, hulking sobs. I choke on my own tears, and I cry some more, and the tears freeze on my hot cheeks. Arpeggio tucks in around my feet. She holds me until I think I am finished and pull away.

"Sorry," I say.

She lifts my chin with two fingers, looks me in the eyes—my pink, swollen, bloodshot eyes—and kisses me. I pull away. *The neighbors are watching us.* But I can't get any further in my thoughts than that.

"Snow's beautiful, isn't it?" she asks. "So quiet and peaceful. It's like God sneezed."

"I guess."

We work together for the longest time, side by side, neither one of us talking, digging and lifting the snow from the driveway.

"If they had gotten lost, and it had started to snow, wouldn't they have found a place to stay? If they were stuck in a snowbank, wouldn't the Staties have picked them up? But there's nothing. Nothing! Nothing but horrible dreams and fear."

"God, Teddy. He really is crazy."

Her words sting. For the last few months, I have been trying to tell her about my dad, at least in some roundabout way, about how nuts he is, how tough he is to live with, how Adrian and I are in a constant dance between the cave of depression and the blaring light of crazy ideas. But now, to hear her say those words, they burn like hot coals. I push the shovel in, lifting way more than she did, lug the weight of the snow to the yard and hurl it over my shoulder.

"Did I say something wrong?"

"No." I lie. "You're fine." Shovel, shovel. Dig, dig. I dig the treacherous steps to the front walk, the shovel clanking against the cracked stone, echoing off the neighborhood houses. I hate this. I hate that she's right, that she knows, that she sees this in me. It's not like I haven't told her. God knows, I've been trying to tell her about my dad for months, but she's never believed me. Always made me feel like I was exaggerating, like I was just feeling sorry for myself. I suck in my pride.

She puts her shovel down and stands in front of me.

"Yes," I say. "He really is crazy." And more hot tears stream down my face. "It doesn't make any sense. My dad—he was doing so much better. He was happy, whistling and singing his stupid tunes. He was eating and cooking. He was making these gargantuan breakfasts. You saw them." I laugh and wipe my nose on my wet glove. "It was like a five-course meal with yogurt and cereal, and then eggs and sausage and potatoes and toast and orange juice. Sometimes he'd even make cookies. I can never eat that much in the morning, but he would cook it anyway. Sometimes he'd pack it up, and I'd bring it for lunch."

"He's a good cook?"

"He's OK. He burns things a lot, because he forgets to turn down the heat, and then he gets distracted. But mostly his stuff tastes—yeah, it's mostly awful."

And now I really laugh, and Evvy laughs with me, and we push our shovels into the snow. The driveway pokes its asphalt nose out as an igloo takes shape on what was once a lawn. I throw a snowball to Arpeggio, and he leaps and twists, catching flakes of it in his lips.

"We need a plan," I say.

"What we need is a car," Evvy says. "Take this matter into our own hands."

CHAPTER 9

———— ⊗⊗⊗⊗ ————

IN SEARCH OF A CLUE

"But, of course," Evvy says, "even if we had a car, where would we go? How would we find them?"

I make scrambled eggs, Evvy makes toast, and Detective Malloy knocks on the front door.

"Mom." I open the door. "The detective's here."

She stands at the top of the stairs, weaving on her heels like she's going to topple over. She's been crying. Her dark circles show even from here. Not sexy or mysterious. "Mom? Do you need some help?"

"No." She blows her nose and wipes her eyes. "Thank you for coming back, Detective. There is something I want you to see."

She grips the handrail and fumbles down the steps, leading him to the kitchen. She points, and he leans over, looking in the refrigerator, pushing things around, now and again saying, "Hmmm," and finally, "What did you want me to notice?"

"Don't you see? There's a whole stick of butter. Gone. And a half a loaf of bread. And here. Look in here." She opens the cupboard.

"Right here. There were three cans of tuna and a jar of peanut butter, and not only that. Forty dollars was stolen from my wallet! He knew I was going food shopping last night. He knew I was getting my paycheck, that I would cash it and go food shopping. He didn't think I'd miss this stuff, but I do. He's been planning this, sitting up nights with what he called 'a grand plan.' But neither me nor Teddy thought about it one way or the other. Did we, Teddy?"

"No, Mom." Did I even know there was a grand plan?

"I've seen these plans before. But at some point, he tells me what they are. He tells me everything. His ideas, his sketches, his notes, his maps. My God. He told me about a cabin in Quebec. But I swear, he gave it up. He promised. No Quebec."

"But he didn't, did he?"

"No. He didn't."

"And you're sure that's what happened? That he kidnapped your son?"

"Yes! Aren't you listening to me? He took the tuna!"

"Mrs. Carson. Please. I have to ask these questions."

"Sorry."

There's that notebook again. "Now. Does he have access to a credit card? Bank account? Anything we can trace?"

"No. He went on a spending spree last fall, and that was the end of that. I cut up his cards. As far as I know, he hasn't been able to get another one."

The detective writes that down.

I can't believe Mom is saying these things to the detective. She's always covered for him, found excuses, made things up. Lying for him is her MO. The fact that she's even alluding to—hell, spilling out—all his craziness is a little scary.

Mom takes the detective upstairs for a more thorough examination of the two rooms. Their voices are muffled, but there is something about what Adrian might have been wearing. Useful information for an ongoing Amber Alert.

Suddenly it all feels very real.

"Kidnapped?" Evvy asks. "That's serious stuff."

"But why?" Words pour out of me. I'm shaking, and I can't stop them. "It's not like a custody case where the father isn't allowed access to his children, where there's a restraining order, a warning, threats with jail. He lives here. He's here all the time. Mom wants him to be involved with us. She begs him to do things with us. Even for my crazy dad, this doesn't make any sense."

Evvy pushes the eggs around her plate. I may not be used to my mom talking about my dad like this, but Evvy is even more uncomfortable. I see it in her like I see it in everyone else who has ever tried to be my friend. They come over after school. We play and do stuff. And then Dad shows up. He lurks in the doorway, larger than life, filling all the air space like some crazy zombie from *Night of the Living Dead*, and my friends are gone. Done. Out of here. But Evvy's been different. She said she loved me. She kissed me under the Guilder Tree, and according to town legend, when you kiss under the Guilder Tree, it means your love will last forever. It's a stupid legend, but I don't care. I believe her. I want to believe her. This stuff—this crazy story of my family—she has to find out sooner or later, but ...

"Do you think they'll find their answers upstairs?" Evvy asks me.

"I don't think so. They may figure out what Adrian was wearing, but I don't know what else."

"Do you think they're going to rope off his room?" she asks.

"I don't know. Why? Do you think we can see something that they can't?"

"Maybe. Might be worth a look. A place to start anyway." She lifts her fork and smiles at me. She can look so sly sometimes.

I grin. My heart melts. She isn't looking to run. She wants to help me, to be with me through this ordeal. "Thank you, Evvy."

Mom and the detective clomp down the stairs.

Detective Malloy sits with us. "That smells good. Who's the chef?"

"Me," I say. "It's only scrambled eggs. Evvy made the toast."

"Eggs can be tricky." He smiles, and there is a pause. Both Evvy and I stare at him. "I have the forensics team looking through their phones, and I'll be calling the FBI in on this case. It's standard in kidnapping cases. Between both phones being left on the sideboard and the missing food and cash, your mother here has convinced me that this is what it is. I don't think Adrian knew what was happening. Tell me again, Teddy—what time did you get up?"

"I think it was about six fifteen. Maybe six thirty. I know it was before Evvy's morning text."

"We check in at six forty-two with the morning wardrobe," Evvy says. The detective smiles awkwardly.

"So, they must have left pretty early in the morning. After five when your mom left for work, but before six fifteen when you got up. Good. Very good. That gives us a window of time. Can Adrian still see light and shadow?"

"Barely. He says he can. But if Dad had the lights on, he could have fooled him into believing it was later than it was."

"Yes. Your dad can be very convincing. This has been a very

hard case for me to wrap my head around. Your dad is charming. Whenever I've talked with him, well, you know your dad. He's always been so interested in my ideas. I had no idea this had been going on. For years, you say?"

I feel slimed. Covered in the shame of mental illness and lies and coverups.

"We'll do what we can, but it's not much, I'm afraid. Like I say, he's a legal guardian. There's no custody battle. It's tricky. But they can't have gone very far on forty dollars. Even with bread and tuna and peanut butter. I'm guessing they're within a hundred-mile radius. It's still a lot of land out here, but they're probably not in Colorado or Quebec. But, well, I'll talk to the boys at the station. On the QT. You know. We have their cell phones, and if there's any clue on there, we'll let you know. OK?"

"OK," I say, and the detective hands me another one of his cards with his work number and even a pager number.

"If you think of anything," he says, "call me."

I look at his card, turning it over in my fingers. "OK."

"And don't, I repeat, *don't* try to solve this on your own. I know he's your dad and it's your brother out there, and if it were me, I'd be feeling a little desperate to do something. But *do not* get involved. From everything your mother has told me, your dad can be a little unpredictable, and I don't want to see you get hurt. So, do your homework. Stay in school. Focus on your own life. OK?"

"OK," I say.

"Evermore?"

"OK," she says.

"Thank you."

He looks at us, or rather, he looks right through us, his steely blue eyes piercing a hole in my forehead. "OK then," he says, and Mom walks him to the door.

"One more thing," he says, the door open, the cold air blowing in. "I've closed Adrian's room and put tape on it. *Do not* go in there."

Damn. "Yes, sir," I say.

And then he is gone, and Mom stands in the doorway, all her courage draining out through her feet. She leans on the doorjamb for a full minute, and then she says, "I'm going to go upstairs and lie down. Will you two be OK?"

"We'll be fine, Mom."

"And, Teddy."

"Yes, Mom?"

"Please. Don't go blabbing this all over the neighborhood. This is hard enough. If word gets out and people start bringing their chickens and casseroles, I don't know what I'll do."

"OK, Mom."

"Thank you." And with that, she is gone. And the house settles one more time into a quiet. I pick up the dishes and carry them into the kitchen. Evvy is at my heels.

"We can't go into Adrian's room?" Evvy asks.

"No," I say. "We've been warned."

"Then we need a new tactic."

"You got any bright ideas?"

We both stand for a full minute, staring at our cold toes. Then Evvy steps in front of me and whispers, "Didn't your dad used to work for Jason Peterson?"

"Yeah. At the Native American Museum."

"I'll bet he knows something."

CHAPTER 10

SOMETHING LIKE A CLUE

In a flash, Evvy, Arpeggio, and I are out the door, shovels in hand, walking to 27 Las Flores, the Petersons' house. Our plan is to offer to clean their walks. Then they'll invite us in for cookies and cocoa. Then we can grill them about ideas. That's the plan anyway.

Evvy can get me to do anything.

The house is tucked up a few streets away in the rabbit warren of streets we call a neighborhood. Around the corner, there's a horse paddock, but today, with the snow and all, they're probably in the barn. Most days, they look happy to be out here—well, as happy as a horse can look with those sad, watery eyes.

These creatures, large as they are, bring a calm to my being. They stand on the earth, solid on four strong legs, and gently, they move through time. They never seem bothered by the issues of everyday life. They walk the trails through the woods, giving people rides, a chance to experience the wonders of nature and an animal. And then they return to the pasture to make quick work of the grass and hay.

The Petersons' house is small, a blue gingerbread house, glistening after the storm. They have shoveled their steps and the walk already, so now we need a new plan.

Jason Peterson was my dad's boss for four whole months, not Dad's best run in the last five years but not his worst either. We moved here from Brattleboro in November, uprooting from one school and landing here in the middle of a semester. Mr. Peterson fired Dad when he hired an Elvis impersonator to entertain for a fundraiser. Dad thought it was brilliant. Would not be talked out of it. No matter what my mom or Mr. Peterson or I said, he was holding his ground. And I don't know all the details, but from what I could gather, the museum rented a huge hall with food for a hundred, and like eleven people showed up. Yeah. They lost money hand over fist in that little gig. At any rate, that was the end of that job, and now I need to find just enough courage to hike up the three neatly shoveled steps to the front door and ring the bell.

Nothing happens at first. No lights flicker on. No footsteps approach the front door. We wait.

A red-tailed hawk glides into the tree beside us. It hunches over, staring at us, eyeing Arpeggio. At forty pounds, Arpeggio is probably too big for a bird of this size. Probably. Hopefully. "Don't look so hungry!" I say, but the bird stares at us.

And then the light comes on, with footsteps close behind, and Mr. Peterson opens the door.

"Yes?"

"Mr. Peterson?"

"Yes."

"I don't know if you remember me. I'm Teddy Carson. My dad worked for you. And ... and this is my friend Evvy Martinez and—"

"I'm sorry. This really isn't a good time for us." He glances over his shoulder into the dark house. "My wife is very sick. Chemo. It makes you very tired."

"Oh. We were going to offer to shovel your walks, but—"

"Jason? Honey? Who's there?"

"It's Sullivan Carson's daughter and her friend ... I'm sorry. What's your name?"

"Evvy."

"Of course. Her name is Evvy. They brought a dog. I'll send them away."

"A dog?" Mrs. Peterson leans on a walker and shuffles into the dining room. Her movements are slow and measured as she lowers herself into the chair and smiles at us. She's still in her nightgown and robe; both are plain blue silk with a little lace on the hem. She holds out her hand, and Arpeggio creeps toward her, step by cautious step. A single tear trickles out of one eye. "It's been so long since we've had a dog in here. Not since the kids were little. Gosh, I've been so sick for so long I've forgotten what joy can do to a person's soul." She rubs Arpeggio from the top of his head to the tip of his tail and says, "Oh, you two are so good to come by. We were talking about getting a dog just this morning, weren't we, Jason?"

He says, "Yes," and nods, and Arpeggio runs back into his arms and licks him upside the face, and he stands up and says, "Where are my manners? Come in. Please. Come in."

The house smells like old cabbage, and I wonder how long it has been since they opened a window, or even a door, to let in some fresh air.

"So, girls, how have you been?" Mr. Peterson sits at the table and folds his hands neatly on his lap.

"We've been OK," Evvy says.

"You seniors now?"

"No. We're juniors. Next year, we graduate."

He nods. "I see." But then he seems to drift off into someplace dark and lonely. I want to say something about cancer and how I've heard it's super hard, and I know what it means to live with depression, and life is harder than it has to be sometimes, but even in my head, it feels shallow. So, we sit together, and he touches Arpeggio, rubs him behind his long, floppy ears, and Arpeggio buries his nose in Mr. Peterson's knees, and the quiet feels quite manageable.

"We haven't had a lot of company lately," Mrs. Peterson tells us. "Jason still works at the museum, going in—how many days are you working now?"

"Three."

"Right. Working three days a week now. The best part is the visits he makes to consult with some of the tribal leaders. So many of these people still live up in the mountains, and it gives him time to drive around. Right, Jason?"

"Yes. Your dad used to do that, but, well, it's funny how things work out. Have you girls been out to look at the leaves?"

"No," I say. "And now with all this snow."

"Oh, yes. I guess it did snow last night. Early, even for here."

"A boy comes to shovel our walks," Mrs. Peterson explains. "It looked like it was a big storm. Was it?"

"About a foot," Evvy says.

"Oh, my," Mrs. Peterson says. "That is big. Yes."

"Do you have any suggestions for where we might go?" Evvy asks. "To look at the leaves? You must know some good places."

"There are so many beautiful places. But now, with all this

snow …" He drifts off again. "Oh heck. It was a freak storm. It should melt in the next day or so. If you—here. June? Make us some tea, will you? I'll show the girls my map."

Mrs. Peterson nods. It takes three tries of rocking back and forth and a steady hand from her husband before she can fully rise and steady herself on the walker. Arpeggio wags and follows her into the kitchen.

"You know"—Mr. Peterson stops at the door of the study, gazing back at his wife—"everything you've heard about cancer is true. Chemo is awful, but you survive. You think you've beat it. You get on with your life. And then it snaps back. Somewhere else. And what you're left with is a depression so wide and so deep it's unfathomable. I didn't think she was going to make it this time."

I want to tell him it's what my dad goes through, too, for like three or four months every year. He says it's like being in a spider's web, and he's the fly, and it's a sticky, paralyzing morass in every direction. My mom begs him to take his meds, any meds, *anything, please*! She threatens to leave him. One time, she even packed her bags. He says he hates them, that they suck a hole in his soul, but after a while, he seems better. At least to us. He whistles and laughs and makes awful jokes that only he and Adrian find funny, but sunlight creeps into the house again. But that's not the worst of it. The worst comes when he goes on a binge, flying from one store to another, spending money we only pretend to have and coming home with a car full of the most useless things you can imagine: gigantic flower vases, antique bicycles, seven sets of dishes. He's so happy, but the last time my mom was so mad she cut up his credit cards and threatened to leave. Again. Course, she never does …

"Teddy? Are you coming?"

"Oh. Yeah. Sorry."

Mr. Peterson's study is lighter than the rest of the house. There is a window open in the corner, and a cold breeze brushes over the snow and wafts in. One whole wall is full of books—the history of the Berkshire region, Native Americans before the white people, Native Americans after the white people, and Native Americans now. Stories. Poems. Songs. Rituals. Every aspect of this complex culture. It's obvious he's been working. Books are piled on the desk. File folders are spread out on a side table.

And on the wall beside his desk, there is a large map of the area.

"You are here," he says and points to Crystal Falls, a tiny dot beside a widening river that flows into the Connecticut River. Now, if you go south toward Stockbridge—that was my mom's people's land, the Mohican People, and her family had a lot"—he squints and points to this teeny spot—"right here. Seventeen of the prettiest acres you'd ever want to see with rolling hills and wildflowers and a pond with lily pads. You can still see it if you go to Stockbridge, although most of it was taken by "eminent domain." White man's lingo for greed. The original peoples set up camp by the rivers. Mohican means the People of the Waters That Are Never Still. Beautiful isn't it?"

I nod. I feel them with us, with Mr. Peterson, in his study, his home, in Crystal Falls. The library and the school and buses rule the streets now, but here, with this man, the ancestors still sing.

"Oh, and then down here, almost to the Connecticut border, that's Great Barrington. You see where I am?"

We both nod. His map is wonderful. It seems most everything is on it, from tiny squares with long, complicated native names, to little churches with steeples, to ice-cream shops, to hiking trails. I don't see any place, though, where Dad might be hiding.

"Yup, and here, there's a state forest. Are you driving yet?"

Evvy shakes her head no, but I say, "I'm in driver's ed at school, and I have my learner's permit. I've been out a few times."

"Yes. That's good. Very good. Well, ask your dad to take you up here. He knows all the little roads, and the colors this year are gorgeous, or they were before the snow. And Monument Mountain—that's this little peak right here—that's a lovely hiking spot. Arpeggio would like that."

"What if we went this way?" Evvy points to the north, toward Adams and North Adams. "What's up there?"

"Well, Mt. Greylock is a beautiful lookout. Climb that, and you can see Vermont, New York, even clear down to Connecticut. You should go soon, though, cause come the end of October, you'll need to watch out for the hunters. They love it up there. My goodness, they come from miles around and stay for days. They're a crazy bunch. In early November, especially, you'll find them all over these mountains."

"Thanks," I say. "Maybe if the snow melts a little, we can get out tomorrow."

"The traffic is insane, but the color will give you a new lease on life. Take a right on Maple Ave out of the center of town. It'll take you up by Warren's Dairy. Good ice cream and Less traffic."

He leads us back to the dining room. Mrs. Peterson has Arpeggio in a sit, and she's feeding him a river of crackers.

"Did Jason show you girls around?"

"I gave them the cook's tour." He's grinning.

We all sit at the table, and Mrs. Peterson pours the tea. The cups are stained on the inside, either coffee or tea. Hard to tell, but it's a little disgusting.

"Where do they stay?" Evvy asks.

"Who?" Mr. Peterson looks at her. Does he remember anything he's said?

"The hunters. The ones that come from miles around," Evvy says.

"Oh." He laughs. "Of course. Well, some of them stay in motels, but most of them, four or five of them will share one of the hunting lodges. There must be fifty or sixty lodges buried in these hills. They're magical little islands, you might say, stocked with food and beer and blankets. Anything you might need."

"Do you have a map of these places?

"Oh, gosh no. They're scattered all over these mountains. From Great Barrington to Mt. Greylock and back again. They're like Dickens's Olde Curiosity Shop. If you're meant to find it, you will. Otherwise, you could look right at it and never see it." He laughs. "You have no idea how big these mountains are till you start driving around them."

We finish our tea and stand up to leave. Evvy gets up first. That's my cue that it's time. "Thank you both so much. This has been so helpful. We will definitely get out and see some leaves. Whatever is left after last night's storm."

"I guess it was a doozey," Mrs. Peterson says as Mr. Peterson stands and walks to the door. "There's a girl in your school. Probably about your age. Sandra Henderson. I think she goes by the name of Tiger. Do you know her?"

"I do," I say.

"She used to ride with your dad sometimes." He stuffs his hands in his pockets. He slumps into his shoulders. "Her grandmother was Mohican, God rest her soul, raised her, and she'd translate for the older people who don't speak English. She was a wonderful volunteer. I'm afraid I haven't seen her for a while."

"She's in my English class."

"Oh. That's nice. Tell her I say hi."

"I will. Thank you," I say.

"Thank you so much for bringing Arpeggio around. Everything seems possible when you touch a dog."

"We'll bring him again, if you want," Evvy says.

We step into the cold sunshine where our trusty shovels await us. The sun slips through the trees, and the sky starts to button up. Night settles in early.

"They sure were glad to see the dog," Evvy says.

"Yes. They were."

We trudge home. I am haunted by the storm clouds that hang over Mrs. Peterson. I've never known anyone else who faced this kind of depression. Not like we do. No wonder my friends would leave and never come back. It's like a wind tunnel, sucking you in, paralyzing you with fear. Arpeggio tugs at the leash, stopping every thirty seconds to inhale the fresh smells. One in particular seems especially interesting, and he snoops around the base of the tree. But then he lifts his head and moves on without even marking it. There is so much I don't understand.

"Evvy? I don't know where to begin. I thought he would tell us, 'Oh yes. Up here. This is one of your dad's favorite places,' and we would go there and find them, and it would all be solved. But did you see that map? Those mountains? It's huge out there. They could be anywhere. What happened? They were here, and now they're gone. Poof. Vanished. Where are they? And what is happening with Adrian?"

"We'll find them. Detective Malloy knows what he's doing."

"You think?"

Evvy squeezes my hand, and for a hot second, I believe her.

"And maybe that girl—Tiger? Is that her name? She might know something."

"Maybe. She barely speaks to me. I'm way not cool enough for her."

"Ask her anyway."

CHAPTER 11

?

Mom and I stand at the sink, shoulder to shoulder, elbow deep in suds and more dishes. Our reflections gaze back at us. We both look like we've been hit by a train. Our faces are drawn and a little gray, and my timing is probably awful, but the question—it pours out of me on its own. I don't know what she will say, but I have to know.

"So, I was in English class the other day."

"And?" She freezes, her hands now glued to the hot water in the sink. She searches her memory.

"Do you remember me talking about Mr. Harrison? My English teacher?"

"Maybe. Why?"

"He, um, he, he's this really cool guy, and—well yesterday, after class, he asked me to stay." I can't believe it was only yesterday. I swear I've aged seventeen years.

"Are you in trouble? Lord Jesus, that's all I need. What have you done now?"

"No, Mom. Honest. It's nothing like that. He's directing a play this fall. Shakespeare. *The Tempest*. And he, um, he asked me to audition." My words are an avalanche with a life of their own. "For this really cool role, Ariel, the fairy, the one who does everything that Prospero asks, all the magic. I was reading about her yesterday afternoon, and I really like it, and I think, gosh, acting. Acting. Me. I never thought I would ever in my life love anything, but think about it, Mom—to be up there, in the lights. I can't explain it."

"And when are these auditions exactly?"

"Next Friday." I swallow.

"And rehearsals are when?"

"After school. I can catch the late bus home and still have time to walk Arpeggio and make supper."

"And who is going to take care of Adrian, if, God willing, he is able to make it home alive?"

My heart sinks. I can't imagine life without my little brother. As much as he's a pain in the ass, he's a funny kid. A blind kid who sees right through me. A smart, dopey ghost whisperer who is always there, in the shadows, by my side, bugging me. Asking questions. Winning my friends out from under my nose. "Do you really think—"

"Yes, I think! I think they should be home! I think your father should have shoveled the driveway. I think we should be having supper together. I think Adrian should be doing homework, playing games on his cell phone, listening to stupid TV. But they're not here, are they? And now it's all I can do to go through the motions of a day."

"I know, Mom."

She leans on the sink, all her weight hanging off her shoulders. She throws the sponge, and dirty water splashes everywhere. "I'm sorry, Teddy. It isn't your fault. I should have known your father would pull something like this. He's been talking about getting away, finding a little cabin in Quebec or Nova Scotia. Someplace far away. But I couldn't let him uproot us again. I just couldn't. I told him that if he needed to go, 'Fine. Go. But I am staying right here.' But Adrian? Taking Adrian? He's a little kid. How could he do that?"

"We'll find them, Mom."

"Well, I'll be damned if I know how." She puts her wet hand on mine. "Oh, Teddy, I'm sorry. I'm sorry to the bottom of my mother's heart, but do you understand what has happened here?"

I don't say anything. I know I should. The words are there. Inside my head: *The falcon cannot hear. Full fathom five. Hunters' lodges. Tuna.* But suddenly none of them make any more sense than a green dolphin with a white belly.

She wipes her hands on a dishtowel and hangs it back on its hook inside the cabinet door. "Teddy. Darling. Listen to me. This is not a play. There may not be a happy ending. Not like you think. We may be dealing with wakes and funerals and hundreds of people stopping by to wish us well and ask us questions that we don't want to answer. Mental illness questions. Blame questions. With looks of how much better they are than us."

I turn away and put water on the stove for tea. I stare at the kettle for the three hundred years while Mom goes on and on about their funerals. The burner turns a hot red, and a fire rises in me from my gut all the way to my eyes. This is probably my only chance to work with Mr. Harrison, and I know that's selfish, and I know that's awful and I shouldn't ever, ever, ever think like this, but I do. I want to do this with my whole selfish heart.

Mr. Peterson is right. These mountains are enormous. It's going to be near impossible to find them out there. Nonetheless I, and maybe

Evvy—I don't think I can do this without her—have to bring Adrian back home. And soon. Before it's too late. I have to be brave.

"Teddy. Come. Sit with me. We need to talk."

I don't move. If I move, I will shake; my courage will dissolve, and I will lose. There will be no Ariel. No *Tempest*. Nothing but Adrian and Dad and this suffocating, strangulating, horrible house. "What happened to him? He wasn't always like this. I remember a time—he would play with us."

She pulls out her grandmother's teapot, the one with Chinese dragons that I love so much that she only uses on the most special occasions, and two tea bags. She finds a tray, takes two cups, a bowl of sugar, and "Milk with your tea?"

"No thanks."

"You're right, Teddy. You're sixteen. It's time you heard what happened."

She pours the hot water into the pot. "Come, my child. Sit with me."

And I do. We sit at the kitchen table, kitty-corner, the mail and laundry stacked at my elbow. She tries to take my hand in hers, but I pull it away, stuffing it into my lap. She leans back and crosses her legs.

"Ever since I called that restaurant and asked to speak to Sullivan's brother, I've been thinking. Can't stop thinking. Your father wasn't always like this. You know, down one day and up the next. Wild ideas. Crazy plans. When I met him, he had such a free spirit, and I fell in love." She drifts through the window over the kitchen sink; some tiny wings carry her through her reflection in the window into a younger time.

"I hadn't wanted to tell you before this. You were so young. I kept telling myself to wait. But gee, Teddy. You're grown up now. You've grown up before your time."

She pours the tea, and the soothing smell of lemon ginger floats into the air. I take a spoonful of sugar and stir it into cup. The steam rises. Mom cradles the cup on her chest.

"Did you know your father had a brother?"

I search my memory, but there is no brother anywhere to be found.

"Yes. Tony. He and your father were the best of friends. They shared a house outside of Las Vegas."

She inhales the steam, fogging her glasses, but she doesn't wipe them off. She talks to me, but she is so far away. I sip the hot tea, but I don't move.

"I was working at Audubon in Nevada. A park ranger. We were both in our late twenties. Your dad—gosh. He was as handsome as the day is long. Tall. Lean. So strong and tanned. He was a manager at one of the restaurants in the casinos, Fantasy Island it was called, with palm trees and parrots. Oh, yes. Real parrots. Dozens of them. Your father hated them, complained incessantly about the racket they made. He would get off at two in the morning, and he and I would drive around the desert looking at the stars and the moon and dreaming of the lives ahead of us. He owned a house with his brother, Tony. Nothing big—a two-family bungalow with a few cacti out front. Tony worked the tables. Neither of us had any idea what was coming."

She bites her lip. She stirs the tea. She wraps her hands around the cup and breathes the steam. She lifts one leg and places it gently over her knee. I wait.

"But one morning, it was still dark, we came home to find the whole thing up in flames. Huge flames, shooting into the sky. The moon was setting, and the sun was poking above the horizon. Tony was in the street. Firefighters were everywhere. But they were too late. Everything was gone.

"'What happened?' we asked. Tony shrugged his shoulders and said, 'Lost it in a poker game. I thought if I burnt it down, we could at least get the insurance. You know. Start over.'"

She doesn't look at me. She puts the cup down.

"Your father never forgave Tony. Never spoke to him again. But he still dreams of that fire. Still wakes up in the night with the terror of those flames. Of everything that was lost."

Now it's me. I take her hands in mine.

"This mental illness, whatever it is that your dad has—the doctors don't know anything, but he has something. It's in his genes. But this night, this fire, this betrayal by his brother—he lost everything. It left him adrift at sea. We started over. We had you, and our lives seemed, well, it all seemed quite happy. You were a blessing for us. For, oh gee. It must have been three or four years. But then, after Adrian was born, everything seemed to change. Your dad would get his feet on the ground, and then something would happen: the fire, the betrayal, the anger, it would all bubble up again.

"He wants his life back, his house on the edge of nowhere. He wants to watch the moon rise over the mountains, to smell the sand and the air, to listen to buffalo stampeding across the wide-open plains."

"What happened to Uncle Tony?"

She refills my cup with fresh, hot tea. "I heard he went to jail. Two years, I think, for arson. And when he came out …" She takes a Kleenex and blows her nose. The tears creep down her cheeks. "Well, we lost touch with him. No one knows what happened. I heard he went to Canada. The Yukon. But I don't know. I don't know if any of this has anything to do with anything, but lately your dad has been muttering about Tony in his sleep. I didn't think anything of it, thought it was another one of his nightmares."

"Do you think he went to Las Vegas?" I ask.

"On forty dollars? No."

"Then where is he?"

She shakes her head. "I don't know. But I'll bet it's someplace where he can see the stars and the moon on a clear night."

CHAPTER 12

STORM IN THE MOUNTAINS

Evvy and I are sipping tea with the Petersons. Arpeggio sits nice and tall in a chair at the table, lapping tea from his own cup. There are four maps spread out on the table—each one on blue paper with scribbles. More are stacked in bright red folders. Mr. Peterson is pointing to this spot up here, a tiny sliver of valley up in the mountains. "Your dad," he says, but I can't hear anything else. Suddenly the cups disappear, and we are outside, blizzard winds ringing in my ears.

"Har the mainsail! These winds are a blowing us out to sea."

Rain batters our little boat. We rock on the waves of the river, and Arpeggio barks at the darkening as clouds sink and rain crashes into the water.

Lightning flashes, its arrows plunging into the water beside us.

Thunder claps, echoing across the mountains.

I call into the wild sky, commanding these elements to silence.

But the storm laughs at us. It lifts our little boat high into the sky, and, in a twinkling, it drops us deep in the river's belly, and we are swimming.

"Evvy? Evvy, where are you?" I call, but it's all bubbles floating to the surface. And just then, a glimpse of her, her toes, floating that way along the current. "Evvy! Come back!" And she tries to turn, but the river carries her out.

I wake up in a sweat.

Sunday is a blur.

Mom says I have to be brave and strong enough for both of us, but I can't, so I tell her I have to do homework and crawl off into my room and try to study. I pick up *The Tempest*. Mr. Harrison and the offer to audition feel so very far away now. I am shipwrecked, like all those characters who are lost on Prospero's island. They all think the others are dead. Ferdinand thinks his dad is dead. Alonso, his dad, thinks that Ferdinand is dead. Antonio wanders around with two clowns looking for a plan. And Ariel, I think— am I reading this right?—is singing invisible songs of woe in each of their ears.

"What R U wearing?"

Oh, God. Is it tomorrow already? "Black. And U?"

The dots on my message app whirl along, but it's a full minute before anything comes back.

"Any news from your dad?"

"No."

It whirls again, and a text message comes screaming in: "Amber Alert: Missing. Adrian Carson. Twelve-year-old white male, five feet four inches, 87 pounds. Last seen Thursday, October 6 at 8:30 p.m.

Presumed taken by his father. Wearing yellow shirt, blue sweater, green pants, red sneakers. Father could be armed and dangerous. Red Mustang, MA.

How did the detective manage this one? I thought his hands were tied.

When we step onto the bus, all conversation stops. The kids wriggle in their seats, gazing out the window at the scenery they have seen every day for the last fifteen years. Of course, they can't show compassion. Not in front of one another. No "Is this your little brother?" Or "How awful for you, Teddy. How are you holding up?"

"Ignore them," Evvy says, and I try to, but their silence and awkward smiles swell inside my head, and there's no room for anything else.

"I can't."

"Then be better than them. Keep your head up and remember what you have to do today," she says. "Talk with Tiger. Find out where your dad might have gone."

In English class, when I open the door, I hear one kid talking about him. "I heard he's a lunatic. Howls at the moon." But he gets poked in the ribs and turns around faster than the lavender knives. I stare at them and start the long walk to the windows.

"That's your brother?" someone finally asks.

"Yeah," I say. "That's my bro."

No one says anything till it bursts out, almost on its own. "Who taught him how to dress?"

Everyone looks at me. I slam my books down on my desk and stare him right in the eye. "He's blind. He can't see color."

And that, miraculously, puts an end to that.

I throw my knees under the little desk and gaze out the window, my mind laser focused on finding my dad and my little brother. I will not cry. I will not cry. Tiger is not here yet. Why not? I will not cry. I will not cry. But—*where are they?* I know people have lived for two days or even a week out in the wild, lost in the woods, wandering in circles around the mountains, surviving storms and freezing temperatures, but I can't imagine either of them faring very well in the elements. The snow. The cold. Are they even alive?

"Yes. Now. Where were we?" Mr. Harrison walks in and fumbles through his briefcase. He takes out his well-worn copy of *The Tempest* and tosses it onto his desk. He paces the length of the room, opening the door and closing it again. Tiger still isn't here.

"Ah, yes. The natural and supernatural world."

Mr. Harrison leans against his desk, pulls an imaginary flute out of his pocket, and begins to play. The room gets really quiet. Imaginary notes bounce off the windows and the walls. He puts the flute in his lap. "Today we must talk about Ferdinand. Poor little Ferdinand," he says, so quietly. "A boy, just sixteen years old, lost on a strange island. He believes with all his heart that his father drowned in the storm. Natural or supernatural?" he asks.

"Natural," we say.

"Are you sure?" Mr. Harrison smiles that all-knowing smile of his. He lifts the flute and begins to play, whistling a simple tune. Then he starts to sing, "This is Ariel, singing to Ferdinand, telling him that his father drowned and his bones now lie deep under water. It's a lonely, grievous song.

Full fathom five they father lies,
Of his bones are coral made:
Those are pearls that were his eyes:
Nothing of him that doth fade,
But doth suffer a sea-change
Into something rich and strange.
Sea-nymphs hourly ring his knell:
Ding-Dong
Hark, now I hear them, ding-dong bell.

He drops his imaginary flute, and like a wind blowing west to east, we all take a breath. I don't know what it means, but it is so beautiful I want to melt away. "Ariel and the flute," he says. "Natural or supernatural?"

"Supernatural."

"Excellent. Prospero is pulling all the strings here, and Ariel is doing his bidding. And this morning, the sprite's task is to convince Ferdinand that his father is 'full fathom five'—drowned at sea, thirty feet under water."

He sings it again, and it starts to open up. The magic, the supernatural. We have landed on this island where nothing is as it seems. Where Prospero, a man of flesh and blood, guides the actions of all the characters. Some by force and threats, like with Caliban; some with promises of liberty and release, like with Ariel; and some with sheer magic, like all those characters who were on the ship. Is he good or evil? I can't say, but I know he's seeking justice for something that happened twelve long years ago.

"Ding-dong," Mr. Harrison sings. "Are you with us, Edwina?"

"Yes. Sorry, Mr. Harrison."

"Thank you. Now …" He puts the flute down and paces the front of the room. He looks at each one of us. "Friday night, there was a storm. It came up out of nowhere, out of a beautiful fall day. Natural or supernatural?"

"Natural," we say.

"Let us hope so." He grins. "And on Saturday morning, who here shoveled the foot of snow?"

A few of us raise our hands.

"Then welcome to the log scene. For today, by Prospero's bidding, poor little Ferdinand must prove himself worthy with an impossible task: move an entire forest of logs from stage right to stage left. Open your books, please. Act three, scene one."

We open our books, rifling through our pages.

"Line 450, please." He stands up and begins to pace, carrying invisible but massively heavy logs across the room. He stops, like maybe he is about to recite some wonderful poetry and fill our hearts with romance. But no.

"It is into this strange and wondrous world that Ferdinand has wandered. Does he know this Herculean task is an old folktale? Clear a forest by sundown? Drink the waters of an entire lake? Spin straw into gold? Shovel a foot of snow from the driveway? Probably not. What he knows, just now, as he turns the corner on the trail, is that standing before him is a beautiful maiden. And who might that be?"

He's looking at me, and just as I am about to answer, Kim's hand shoots into the air.

"Miranda," she says, though he doesn't call on her.

"Thank you, Kim. Yes, the young and lovely Miranda, daughter of Prospero. And after twelve long, lonely years on this island, gazing only upon the wretched, hideous, deformed Caliban or the fairy nymph, Ariel, suddenly there, before her very eyes is a man. A real man. A prince. And what does our sweet, innocent Miranda see?"

We skim the lines. "Edwina? Can you read please?"

I clear my throat: "'I might call him / A thing divine, for nothing natural / I ever saw so noble.'"

"Natural or supernatural?" he asks, and this time, we don't know what to say. I thought we were getting the hang of this, but—"Edwina?"

"Well, it must feel like magic when suddenly, out of nowhere, a man, well, a boy, really, but what the heck—a guy. A real flesh-and-blood guy shows up."

The door opens, and Tiger stands there. She yells at someone we cannot see, "Yeah? Don't you ever, I mean ever, touch my brother again, or you'll be sorry your mamma ever made you. There's a reason why they call me Tiger!" And she closes the door behind her. "Oops. Sorry, Mr. Harrison."

"Sandra Henderson. How nice of you to join us. Please. Take your seat." Mr. Harrison smiles at her. "You good?"

"It's Tiger. Sir. And yes. I'm fine." Tiger dumps her bag on her desk and slides into her seat. She crosses her arms and sighs. "I hate bullies," she hisses under her breath. "Where are we?"

"Act three, scene one," I whisper, and show her the page.

"Exactly, Edwina. A real flesh-and-blood guy. Thank you." Mr. Harrison opens the door and looks down the hall, but whoever was there is gone. He returns to the front of the room. "A thing divine." He goes to the whiteboard and writes *natural* and *supernatural* in big capital letters. "Natural, remember, is what we can see and hear. Supernatural is—how shall we define the supernatural? Anyone?"

We sit in silence for the longest time. None of us daring to move or speak out. Supernatural. It seems so obvious. It's magic. It's wonder. Finally, Tiger puts her hand up.

"Sandra? Sorry. Tiger?"

Tiger smiles and snaps her gum. "The supernatural, well, for Shakespeare, is the theater. Right?" Snap. "You said this was Shakespeare's last play. His farewell to the stage. Isn't the supernatural, then, the magic of stage? The thunder machines? The flute of Ariel?"

Mr. Harrison puts his hands together over his heart, and he bows to her. Wow!

"Yes. Thank you, Tiger." He turns back to the whole class. "Miranda and Ferdinand are not like Romeo and Juliet. Those two were passionate, hungry teenagers, ready for whatever love and life would throw at them. Their bodies were fire, the sun and the stars, the moon and the planets. They were drawn together like magnets. But Miranda and Ferdinand—these two are everything sweet and charming and adorable. Miranda says, 'If you say you love me first, then I'll say I love you, too.' And 'Oh heaven, oh earth, bear witness to this sound.'" And Mr. Harrison becomes a sixteen-year-old boy, a prince who curtsies a little, twisting his foot in an embarrassed kind of way. "And this is where natural and supernatural meet, where Ariel pipes his pipe and sings his songs and love melts before our eyes. And so, ding-dong, the bell doth strike for the next class."

"Tiger. Wait!" I call, but she's already halfway out the door and into the crowded hall.

CHAPTER 13

DRIVING

I get to driver's ed. "Sandra Henderson." The teacher tosses her a set of keys. "You're on."

"I'm driving?"

"You sure are. And Edwina Carson. You're in the car! Come on, you two. Let's go."

Tiger takes first shift behind the wheel. She's so smooth. She backs out of the parking space, and the car cruises into the neighborhood. For twenty minutes, she stops at the yellow light and goes on the green; she stays in her lane, stretching out for bicyclists; and when she gets to a straightaway, she rolls down her window, rests her elbow on the edge, and relaxes into a smooth, easy ride. The sun is warm. A cool breeze brushes over the snow and floats in. The fresh air feels good on my face.

"Tiger?" I say as casually as I can. "Is your bother OK?"

"Yeah." She snaps her gum. "Some kid tried to steal his sneakers this morning. He was just about to wrap them around the telephone wires, but I showed him." Snap. "Guess they didn't get the memo about no more freshman hazing."

"Wow. I ... uh ... I think you know my dad."

"I do?" She looks at me in the rearview mirror.

I'm stumbling over all my words, pushing myself to be cool here. "Sullivan Carson. I ... I think you rode with him for the museum."

"Sully Carson is your dad?"

"He is."

"Take this next right up here," the teacher says. "And use your blinker. That's good. Slow around the corner. Very nice. You've been driving for a while?"

"About a year. My boyfriend lets me take the wheel sometimes."

"Oh. Really? Even before you had a learner's permit?" she asks.

"It's always safe." Tiger snaps her gum and looks at the teacher. "You know, empty parking lots, back roads. Easy stuff."

"Eyes on the road, please."

She looks at me in the rearview mirror. "Gosh, Teddy. Sully Carson. Yeah, I rode with him for most of the winter and into the spring. We went all over these mountains. Wow. He's your dad? You are so lucky." Tiger rubs her heart. "He's such a wonderful man. You know, the way he listens. He would always make me feel like I was the most important person on the planet. And he asks the most interesting questions, you know. Questions that really made me think about my life. He helped me to break up with my old boyfriend. Yeah. Wow. He's your dad? I loved riding with him."

There are so many people who say this to me—tell me what a swell guy my dad is. And it's always the same: the way he listens. The way he makes them feel so important. But not me. Not Adrian.

"We used to sneak off sometimes, go to this dairy farm, Warren's I think it was called. Yeah, that's it. Warren's Dairy. They make their own ice cream and milkshakes. They had a petting zoo with chickens and goats, and even in January, on a warm day, we would sit on the bench and gaze across the foothills and the mountains. We were in the presence of infinity. Of God. I was so sorry to hear he was let go. How is he doing?"

"He's doing good," I lie. "I mean, he was bummed about losing that job, but yeah. He's good."

"Carson," the driving teacher says. "Carson. Are you the same Carson as the Amber Alert?"

I swallow. Hard. "Yeah. That's my little brother."

"I'm sorry to hear that. How are you holding up?"

"OK." I give it my best shot at a smile.

"Do you want to drive?" Tiger asks. "Because it's probably your turn to spin the wheel."

She pulls the car over to a shoulder of the road. We're on a back road, God knows where, but there is no traffic for miles around. I step into the driver's seat and snap my seat belt into place. The teacher guides me through every move. "Check your mirror. Ease onto the road. Steady now. Thirty-five miles an hour is a good speed. Stay steady."

I grip the wheel and squeeze onto the road. I glance in the rearview mirror. Tiger is staring out her window. She opens her phone, and the screech of the Amber Alert comes back up.

"Very nice, Edwina. Hold her steady. Think of the car like a ship: hold her steady in a storm."

I grip the wheel and step on the gas, and then I ease up, and this ship moves in fits and starts. The teacher clings to the dashboard until I manage to get it moving.

I drive for what seems like hours, my hands sweating on the wheel, my foot shaking on the gas. I slam on the brakes when anyone gets near me. Finally, I creep back through town and pull into a parking spot behind the school.

"Hey," Tiger says. "I am sorry about your bro. But if he's with your dad, he'll be fine."

"Thanks, Tiger. I'm sure you're right."

CHAPTER 14

KIM

I squeeze through the crowd headed toward the cafeteria. I look around for Evvy, but our table is empty. The line for pizza is slower than slow, and I open my phone and text: "Are u at lunch?"

I wait. And inch forward in the line. And wait some more. My heart is racing. Everyone is looking at me as the girl from the crazy family.

"There you are," Evvy sneaks up behind me and whispers in my ear. "I have some lunch. Do you want to go to outside?"

"Outside?"

"It's gorgeous out there. We can watch the snow melt."

We have twenty-two whole glorious minutes all to ourselves, and we find a dry bench in the sunshine around the side of the building. It's quiet out here, and the sun is warm. One day, we get a foot of snow; two days later, it's sixty-five degrees in the sun. Go figure that one out.

There are only a few cars on the little side street. Mostly, it's neighborhood, though why anyone would want to live across from the high school is beyond me. Still, there's a pretty little yellow house with a blue birdfeeder that is awash with cardinals, goldfinch, and a few stray pigeons, some of whom have also figured out that we have sandwiches. They stop by to say hi. Arpeggio would like nothing better than to run through the middle of them, making them flap their wings and take to the sky.

Evvy opens a folder and pulls out some watercolors. "So, I was working with this kid this morning in art class, a really smart kid but super shy—I think he's gay and terrified, but I don't know how to ask him, so instead, I worked with him on his image of Ariel. He's amazing, Teddy. You should talk to him. Tell him your ideas for Ariel. When you get the part, of course. He says that Ariel has magic, even in the toes!" She shapes her fingers like dragon toes. "So, look. Can you see the tufts of fur in the toes? Oh yeah. One quick flick of the toes, and flowers will bloom on the hillside!"

"You really think I'll get the part?"

"I know so. He asked you to audition. He senses what you can do." She rifles through the watercolors and pulls out a second one, this one of Ariel conjuring the storm.

"That's great," I say, and I mean it, except I don't. I can't try out for this part. I can't do anything. I can never leave my house. I am stuck there, a coyote in a trap, so close to freedom and so very far away. "But listen, I rode with Tiger this morning," I say, changing the subject. "In driver's ed."

"OMG! Yes. I was so wrapped up in these images I totally forgot. Here. This is for you." She pulls out a cheese sandwich with mayonnaise and lettuce and hands me half. She opens a small bag of potato chips. "And these are for us," she says, and I take one. They are the

best potato chips I have ever eaten—crisp and not too salty. She smiles
at me, and everything about her is in that smile: our months together
as friends, our time inching toward that kiss under the Guilder Tree.
And now my brother's disappearance. She fishes in her bag and pulls
out a map. "So. Back to the plan. Tell me about Tiger."

"She thinks my dad is the greatest thing since the Ringling
Brothers—of course, everyone does—but somewhere in all of her
adulation, she did mention Warren's Dairy, an ice-cream place where
she and my dad would go sometimes. They'd sit on a bench and gaze
over the mountains into the eyes of God. I think it's on the road toward North Adams. Somewhere."

"Do you think it might be a clue?"

I laugh. "Considering how much we have to go on, it could be."

Evvy clicks on the maps on her phone and traces the routes to
North Adams. "Routh 91? That's the interstate. Or this one? Route
5? Or these little back roads?"

I'm just about to describe in delicious, comic detail how Tiger
snaps her gum, like all the time, and how pensive she looked gazing
out the window of the back seat, but before I can start, Theo and Kim
from my English class pop up in front of us.

"Hi, Teddy."

"Hi, Kim. Hi, Theo."

"I'm Kim. From your English class."

"I know." The sun is in my eyes, and I have to shield my eyes and
squint.

"Mr. Harrison says you might try out for Ariel in *The Tempest*. Is
that true?"

"Maybe," I say.

"Oh." She's so perky. "Gee. Cause he asked me and Theo to try out for Miranda and Ferdinand. You know, the romantic couple." She giggles and curls into Theo, who twirls the notes up and down on his harmonica. They're disgusting.

"Isn't he adorable?" Kim squeaks.

"The cutest," I say.

"But you know Caliban, don't you? Ariel's kind of, sort of brother on the island? Prospero's deformed half-beast prisoner?"

Theo twists himself into a knot and claws the air, growling and hissing through his harmonica, a sound like trees cracking under the weight of a heavy wind. He gives me the creeps.

"Isn't he adorable?"

"You asked me that already," I say, and Evvy kicks my ankle. "Yes." I grit my teeth. "Totally."

I've never seen Theo like this. He's always been the better-than-the-cool-kids-snob, haunting the shadows with his creepy harmonica. I imagine him most nights wrapped in a smoking jacket, reading Russian novels and playing chess with the ghost of Dostoyevsky, a glass of bourbon on the table beside him and a cigar burning in the ashtray: ahhh ... the omens that come in smoke and ashes. White Bishop to E4.

Kim chirps on: "Mr. Harrison told me I should read the whole play three times, and I did, and then Theo and I read it together. It was so much fun. And we were going to audition for Miranda and Ferdinand, but when I was reading the play again last night, well, I think that Ariel is such a cool character, you know, Prospero's lieu-tenant, the one with all the magical powers, and I was thinking—would you mind if I tried out for it too? Cause Theo said that if I got the part of Ariel and he got the part of Caliban, he would play the harmonica for me. I mean, if I got the part, of course. He would be like Ariel's magic flute. Isn't that the coolest idea?"

I take a deep breath, my stomach catching in my throat.

"And my mom said she would pick me up after rehearsal, and we just got a new SUV, and she said she would carpool kids home after rehearsals. Isn't that neat?" She looks at Theo again, this ugly grin stretching across her face.

"Hey. Suit yourself," I say. I throw a wet snowball across the street, and the finch go flying.

"Oh, that's great. Thank you, Teddy. I'm going to practice that song—you know, the 'Full Fathom Five.' It's such a pretty song." And then she flounces off, with Theo in tow.

I clench my teeth. "She'll probably get it too." If I didn't hate her so much, I'd probably think she was adorable. The way some girls think dolls are adorable. But I just want to pull her hair.

"Teddy?" Evvy pulls my spirit back to the bench. "Did you ask your mom?"

"I did. She said no. Well, not in so many words. She said we have a few other things going on right now." I throw my bread crust, and seven pigeons flap into position. "I hate him." I spit.

"Who?"

"My dad, of course. Even when he's not around, he runs my life. I'm sixteen years old. I want something for myself here. But then, get this. After she said no? Oh, she was so nice. We had tea, and she tried to tell me what a wonderful guy my dad used to be. Before it all went south. I'm sorry, Evvy. I know I'm not supposed to feel like this, but …"

Evvy takes my hand in hers and kisses it. "Ouch," she says, and her voice is soft and smooth.

"Yeah. It stinks. I'm completely under her thumb. She tells me I have to do something, and I have to do it. I can never see any way out of it. So, I do it. But the more I do for her, the more she makes me do."

"It can't be as bad as that."

"You've never seen my parents in action. Anyone who has known them knows it's as bad as that."

"Teddy. Stop. They're your family. You love them. I know you do."

I look at Evvy's face, and I see her fear. Her fear like my fear, that I am incapable of ever loving anyone. And the fear oozes all the way to my bones. The wall that I've built around myself, this fortress that I think will protect me—it's killing me. I'm choking on my own fear. *When I get free*—I think, so I say, "You're right. It's not that bad. Adrian is one of the sweetest, most wonderful kids ever, and I have no idea where he is, and I'm supposed to wait patiently while Detective Malloy works his magic. But I don't see no rabbit coming out of his hat, do you? I hate this. I hate everything about this." I stand up and gather my things.

"Wait." She stands and takes my hand. "You know, Teddy, it's funny. I know your family has lots more money than my family has, but—"

"I know. I know. Money can't buy happiness."

"That's not what I was going to say. I was going to say that I think it's easier at my house. Don't take this the wrong way, OK?"

Now I am nervous.

"Whatever issues we have, and I know we have them, we're not crippled by them. I think that's what you've been trying to tell me about your family. That the problems they have are inside." She touches her heart. Then she touches mine. "Here."

My lip starts to quiver.

"And that can't be easy."

We walk back to the door, and she's right. Everyone in my family is a prisoner of my father. Even my mom. She's his prisoner too. We all have to bend to his moods and his needs and his whims. For all the times I've imagined him getting shipped off, put away somewhere, disappearing off the face of the earth—what did I want? Did I want for my mom to need me? To lean on me for strength and wisdom? Well, now I have it.

"A penny for your thoughts." Evvy opens the door for me.

I look into the dark lobby and the dark halls beyond that. I know I'm wandering through a labyrinth. "I'm just thinking about what it means to love," I say.

"The way you love me, you mean?" She looks at me with this silly, sheepish grin.

"Oh heaven. Oh earth," I say. "'Bear witness to this sound!' And you? What are your thoughts?"

"I think we need to find your brother."

"Yeah. I think we need a car."

CHAPTER 15

RED

It starts with a sound, distant and faint. A maple tree rustles in the soft breeze. A cardinal trills in a nearby tree. A rose petal falls from the vine. And then it is close, as close as my ear on your chest, your hand on my heart. Your blood courses through your veins, circling, gurgling, pushed along by your pulse.

You take my hand and lead me down a long, dark hall to a small room with a small window high in the wall. A yellow desk perches in the corner.

Red is time moving forward.

Red is a red folder on the yellow desk, pale blue papers spilling out: maps, notes, a silver compass. My hand turns the compass over. It has no weight. Its needle spins. North. West. North Adams. Behind me, a door creaks. I turn and look.

Red crackles. A fire in an empty fireplace. Hot sparks spit into cold air. A small window. Black sky beyond. Silver stars cling to the canopy. And the warm glow of your face when you look at me. Your eyes are deep brown, your lips are pink and tempting, your cheeks glow. My heart beats in every corner of my body. The heat swells within me.

I wrap my arms around my knees. I want this night with you, this night at this fire, at this cabin, in this dream. I sink into your warm glow as the sun creeps over the eastern ledge, pouring thin pink rays into my room, coming at last to rest on my soft bed.

Arpeggio stirs, and I slip into consciousness.

"Oh heaven. O earth."

CHAPTER 16

A NEW ME

The house is quiet. Mom must still be asleep. I don't turn the lights on. I kiss Arpeggio and scratch him behind his ears—his soft spot— and tell him to be as quiet as a cat. We tiptoe down the long, dark staircase, Arpeggio at my feet. It's all I can do to find the steps.

I click on the lights to the basement stairwell, and the room flickers with blue fluorescence. Arpeggio and I creep down to the cellar, step by step. I know from experience that the third step squeaks in the middle, so I count and step over to the side, pointing and helping Arpeggio to do the same. I grip the bannister. Step by step.

It's a finished basement that no one ever uses, so it feels hollow and empty and cavernous. It isn't that big. There are four little windows around the room, with a view of Mom's shrub roots outside. Very little natural light comes in. We have a TV down here, but Mom didn't want to pay for the extra cable, so all we get are two channels on rabbit ears. And the couch is so full of dust that when I sit on it, I break out in hives. The laundry room is over there, under one of the windows. The ironing board is right next to it, but no one wants to iron, so we throw our clothes onto the kitchen table, fold them after a fashion, and wear them with wrinkles.

Arpeggio follows me into the furnace room. I switch on a light, and another dim bulb flickers. Machinery chugs and wheezes. Dust kicks up: dry, moldy, old—book dust that fills my nose and leaves a taste of stale fish in my mouth. There are footprints in the dust. Dad's footprints, so I know we're close. I can feel the warmth of being close. Dad is whistling in these boxes, the lost ones, stuffed and forgotten behind the furnace. There are like seven of them. Boxes of art and books and knickknacks. The tape holding them closed is long gone. I open the first box and fish around inside. It has Dad's old record collection. LPs from a hundred years ago: Rolling Stones. Beatles. Joni Mitchell. Does he think they're worth something now? The box weighs a ton and half. No wonder they went the way. Arpeggio stands at my shoulder and sniffs them. I push the box away and reach for another.

"They're called records. Yeah. Now shh. Very quiet, puppy. We're down here because we have to find Adrian, and last night I had a dream, and if we can find where Dad stashed his notes … then we'll have another clue. Two clues. Three, actually." I hold out my index finger and count. "One: there is his job at the museum and all the routes he took around these mountains, interviewing the native peoples about their culture." I flick out my middle finger. "Two: there are those gazillion little hunting lodges scattered hither and yon. The ones Mr. Peterson talked about." Ring finger. "Three: there's Tiger and their trips to Warren's Dairy." I push the second box away and pull the third one in close. "Too bad we don't know anything." This box has old books. Big books, nature books mostly. And photographs. Some that Mom took. A black-and-white image of a waterfall somewhere. Another of a great horned owl in a tree. They're pretty good.

"Can you smell fresh Dad in any of these boxes?"

Arpeggio puts his nose in the boxes with the books, pawing and sniffing. I don't think he knows what we are looking for, but the comfort he brings is incredible. I push that box aside and pull another one in. When I open this one, I find it.

Right on top.

A red folder. With blue pages.

"Oh, Arpeggio, 'this is the stuff that dreams are made of.'"

I tuck the folder under my arm and put all the boxes back where I found them. Arpeggio and I have made trails of dust with our feet and the boxes, and if the detective comes in here, he'll know for sure we were here. But there's nothing I can do about it. We turn the light off, and the room goes dark and hollow.

We creep up the stairs and open the door to the kitchen.

"Good morning, Teddy."

Mom sits at the table, her hands wrapped around a cup. The tea steams. She looks about eighty years old. Her skin sags. Her eyes are very far away. I stuff the red folder into my pajamas. Mom is so out of it, she doesn't even notice. "Hi, Mom. You're up early."

I go to the back door and open it, real cool and innocent like. Arpeggio looks at me. "No," I tell him. "I'm not coming. You go out," and he slinks outside. I stand at the sink, looking out the window as he shifts from bush to tree, sniffing. My heart fills with love for him.

"The detective called. Woke me up. No one answered the Amber Alert. Can you believe it? No one saw anything. They checked all the hospitals again, stretching out to a two-hundred-mile radius. He told me again that his hands were tied, that his boss threatened to take his badge if he continues to interfere in 'a domestic situation.' And, of course, there's still no sign of your father. The detective says that's good news, that they're probably still alive, but I don't know." She rubs her temples. "Oh, and he said the forensics guys managed to get into his phone. There were calls to Las Vegas. Seven. Maybe eight. But no more than that. And those only lasted thirty or forty seconds. No contact. Anyway, he's going to trace the calls and get back to me." She holds her head in her hands.

"You look tired."

"I am. I have a terrible migraine. Stress, I think. I haven't been sleeping well."

"I'm not surprised," I say.

"How are you, honey?" she asks.

"Me? Gosh. I'm …" I think fast. "I'm scared. Yeah. I'm scared for both of them, but I'm really scared for Adrian. Poor kid. He's only thirteen years old. A little kid. I know he's the smartest kid in the whole world, but how is he supposed to make sense of what is happening? And there's so much that we just don't know ourselves."

Mom nods. "You're a wise kid, Teddy."

I'm totally flummoxed by this compliment. This is a mom I haven't seen in a long, long time. The one who has been around is the one who has been taking care of my dad, holding together the threads of this family, always a failure, always angry, always on the edge of tipping into the bleak unknown. Except that she can't. Because who would take her place?

"Thanks, Mom," I say. Maybe I'm supposed to say something else, but I can't think of what it might be. And maybe I'm supposed to trust her when she says that things will be different from now on.

Yeah. And maybe, just maybe, Jesus will come back, and world peace will be a given, and climate change will solve itself.

I open the door, and Arpeggio comes back in. What a good dog he is. I scratch him behind his ears, and he curls into my knees. I grab his bag of dog food and dump some in his bowl. "Sit," I say, and he sits, tall and proud, swishing his stumpy little tail across the floor. "OK! Good dog." He sniffs his foods and then begins, picking up his kibble, one at a time, chewing and swallowing each one. His little tail still wags, and his tags ring against the edge of his bowl.

"Can you get yourself ready for school this morning? My headache medicine is starting to kick in. I should go to bed before I fall asleep at this table."

"Of course, I can. I'll be fine."

"OK then. I'll see you this afternoon." She reaches for the doorjamb and steadies herself.

"Can I borrow the car?" I ask. "Since, you know, since you'll be asleep, and it would be so cool for me with all the kids on the bus. They could watch me drive by, and I would wave out the window and——"

She leans and turns to me. "Don't be ridiculous. You only have your learner's permit. Understood?"

"Yes, Mom."

"Good." She sighs. "I don't know what I'll do when I do have to go back to work. I'm not sure I can face it."

"You'll be ready, Mom. You'll be fine."

"Thanks, honey."

I listen to her footfall, one step at a time. Her bedroom door creaks open and then latches shut.

And then I am up the stairs, Arpeggio clinging to my shadow, and back in front of my mirror, donning black leggings, a black turtleneck, and a red sweatshirt. "This is the color of fire," I tell Arpeggio. "The color of love."

"Shh." I signal for him to come, and he leaps from the bed. I grab my book bag on the way out the door, my phone, my notebook, *The Tempest,* and the red folder. Back in the kitchen, I grab the last jar of peanut butter and celery sticks. I listen. "Shh," I say again, and Arpeggio sits tall and quiet.

"She's asleep."

Her purse is on the kitchen table. I can't believe I am doing this, but I open her purse, open her wallet, take out twenty dollars and her car keys.

"Come on, pup. We've got work to do."

The basement light flickers again. We step aside at the third step and open the door to the garage. Arpeggio hesitates. Damn. He knows this is wrong. "Come!" I hiss. He tucks his little tail and crawls out. I open the car door and signal for him to get in, and he does, curling up on the front seat like a beaten animal. I open the garage door. *So quiet.* Mom's room is just above. Two stories up. I wait. I listen. Nothing.

I get in the car, close the door, snap my seat belt, start the engine, and slide the car out of the garage, into the driveway, and down to the street. My heart pounds in my chest, and my temples throb. My foot shakes on the accelerator. My hands sweat bricks. Every muscle that can shake is shaking, but I drive out of the hood and onto Main Street, following the route that is going to take me into town and to the school.

CHAPTER 17

———— ∞∞∞ ————

ROAD TRIP

"What's this?" Evvy leans in through the open window.

"It's a car."

"Duh. I figured that."

"Hop in. We're going to go find Adrian."

"OMG!" She opens the door and slides in, kissing me gently on the cheek. "You heard from him? You know where he is?"

"Well, not exactly. But I had a dream last night, and my dream led me to my dad's notes, and I think if we follow them, plus the clues we have, we'll figure something out."

"Well, OK then. Let's do this. Let's go find your brother. And yes, hello, Arpeggio. I do see you."

Arpeggio wriggles in between the seats, wagging his little tail, his nose open and ready for Evvy's sweet kisses. She delivers.

"Hop in the back, Arpeggio," I say, but he looks at Evvy, his deep, watery eyes peering into her light brown, tender eyes, and he leans against her so she can scratch behind his ears.

"Dare I ask?" She scratches his ears. "Whose car is this?"

"My mom's."

"You can't be serious. She said it was OK? That you could borrow her car? Even though you only have a learner's permit?"

"She did," I lie and try to smile, gripping every trembling muscle. "She said I was definitely ready to take it out on my own."

"That is so incredibly fabulouso. Teddy, my beloved, you are the bomb."

I promised Evvy that I would never lie to her, and now I have done it, and even if I have done it for a really good reason—so that we can go find Adrian—it's still a lie. Well, maybe it's only an exaggeration of the truth. Because after all, Mom took a sleeping pill. For her headache. And that should knock her out for eight hours. Which gives us till six o'clock tonight. Plenty of time to find him and get back. She'll never know.

"Teddy? Your hands are shaking. You OK?"

"Yeah," I lie again. My heart is throbbing in my temples, and my hands are sweating like tsunamis, but "I'm OK. It's my first time driving like this is all. I'll be OK. After all, I'm the bomb, right?"

"Right. So, where do we start?"

"Warren's Dairy. It's the ice-cream place that Tiger told me about. If that place was as important to Dad as Tiger thought it was, and if someone there saw Adrian and my dad, then maybe we can get a clue about where they were going. We'll have a trail."

"That's a lot of ifs."

I ease the car onto the street, looking first in one mirror, then the other, then turning around to look behind me. Hands at ten o'clock and two o'clock. Foot on the gas. Easy. And then we are gliding along. A car pulls up behind us. I watch it. I stare at it in my mirror. My hands fill with sweat again, and my heart pounds. *What if it's a cop? What if he knows? What if my mom called, and they're out looking for us?* I breathe. Slow. Deep. Breaths. I turn right onto Main Street, and the other car turns left. Breathe.

I'm sixteen years old. Maybe not all grown-up but almost. I can do this. I can stop at yellow lights, wait for the green, inch forward with the traffic, and stay in my own lane. It's not that hard.

We turn onto the road to North Adams. The town drifts away. The traffic eases up. Evvy gazes out the car window into the soft morning breeze wafting around us. The mountains loom large in the distance, like Oz—just beyond those poppy fields. A hawk floats on the wind. Everything smells like wet earth, piles of leaves, melting snow, fresh grass.

It feels like one minute, maybe twelve, and we are staring at a billboard for Warren's Dairy.

"This is the place?" Evvy asks.

"I think so." I turn left into the driveway, navigating up a steep, narrow lane into a parking spot in the middle of the lot.

"Want a cheeseburger?" I open the door, and Arpeggio leaps out, chasing a chipmunk into a tree. The animal glares down from the first branch, chirring and flicking its tail.

There is an enormous red barn with a window for ordering. There are picnic tables and benches and a fenced-in area with chickens and goats. One of the goats is black with a thin white tuxedo stripe down its chest and long, floppy ears. It looks like Arpeggio only bigger. The dog stares at the goat, and the goat stares at the dog. "Do you think they know they look alike?" I ask.

Evvy shakes her head. "Life is a mystery. A beautiful, wonderful mystery." She gazes on the horizon.

What Tiger said about this place is true. I stand beside Evvy looking at the mountains. The fog makes everything soft and mythic. This is what forever looks like, both in time and in space. We stand on this ancient land where so many people before us have stood, each one of us from the beginning of time till now, at the edge of inspiration. I wonder how many of them found it here. The answer to their prayers. I wonder if my dad did.

"That's why people call these mountains the American Mount Olympus. They're full of ancient gods and spirits." A soft breeze rustles through the yellow leaves. The sugar maples are turning red, almost before our eyes.

Evvy takes my hand and squeezes it. "This is the place where your dad would come with Tiger?"

"I think so. From her description, this is it."

"It's beautiful."

At the edge of the parking lot, a trail leads out down the steep hill, and down that way, there are pine trees and a pond. The hawk reappears, soaring overhead. We stand in silence, mesmerized by the enormous sky that drapes this landscape. We are in the presence of God. Our hearts beat together; our two breaths are one breath. Invisible yet there. Together. They intertwine and float off toward the west. I edge in closer to her, my arm brushing up against hers, and warm air runs up my spine. Evvy wraps her arm around my waist. In the soft October light, she is beautiful. She is here, with me, on this wild adventure to find my little brother somewhere up here in these mountains. I want nothing more than to throw caution into the wind like a kite, to take her in my arms and kiss her, long and deep.

"Do you think they were having an affair?" Evvy asks.

The question takes me completely by surprise. It probably

shouldn't. Between Mr. Peterson and Tiger, I probably should have suspected something, but this puts it into words. Real flesh-and-blood words. My bones fill with water as, once again, this tender moment between us passes. The moment always passes. "Who?"

"Your dad and Tiger, silly."

"I … I don't—I … I just can't imagine it, you know? I mean. He's my dad."

"I know. But do you think they—"

"The cheeseburgers smell good," I say. "Want some lunch?"

"You have money?"

"A little," I say. "Enough for a couple burgers and maybe a fries."

By the time we get to the window, we've changed our minds three times about what we want. Evvy orders a hot dog and chocolate milkshake. Two cups. I order a cheeseburger and a small fries. Two plates. Lots of ketchup. I order a hamburger, no bun, and a bowl of fresh water for Arpeggio. Twelve dollars and seventy-five cents. I leave the quarter in the tip jar.

Evvy wanders, lost in thought. I pull out my phone to see if Mom has woken up, but there is no cell service up here, so I go back to the window and whip out a picture of Dad and Adrian.

The guy at the window stares at the phone. "So?"

"So?" I click my tongue and shift my weight. So, what else could I be asking? "So, have you seen these two dudes? It would be last Friday. Probably in the morning."

"You a cop?"

I laugh. "Do I look like a cop?"

He looks at me, and then he looks at the picture. "Sorry," he says. "But I wasn't working last Friday. Hey, Larry? There's a lady out here. Wants to know about a couple guys."

Larry steps outside. He looks at the picture. Looks at me. "That your dad? You don't look like him."

"It's still my dad. You see him?"

"Why. He missing or something?"

"I … um … he said he was at work. Um. Mom thinks he was … um … playing hooky. She sent me out to spy on him." I smile my most innocent smile.

The guy smiles back, his dingy teeth hanging in the air. "I did. He was here with a weird little kid. Yeah. That kid. Kept hopping on one foot and laughing. Not like something was funny though. More like something was, I don't know, new, I think." He points to the picture. "They sat at that table over there for, gee, maybe an hour? Seemed strange, as it was getting pretty cold by then."

"Did you see which way they went when they left?"

"No. Sorry."

The first guy comes back. "Here's your food."

Evvy and I sit at the picnic table. Arpeggio sits at our feet. The three of us sit in silence and look out over the Pine Tree Trail. A hill, pine trees. And way down there in the pond are teeny tiny ducks and two white blobs. Swans. Yeah. They must be swans. They're moving. Beyond it, mountains melt into reds and yellows as the sun rises high in the sky. Everything is so far away. The red of the maple trees reflects in the water, and pink light spreads across the pond at the bottom of the hill. Try as I might, I cannot get the images of him and Tiger out of my head: *Could he? Would he? Did he go slow with Tiger? Touch her skin, make her rise? Was there passion? Did he wonder? Were we ever in his thoughts?* I shake it off.

Evvy sucks up the last of the milkshake. I lick the ketchup off the back of my hand. The sticky, sweet flavor—I nearly forget why we're here. "So, now what?"

"Well, here's what I know: they were here. The guy inside recognized their picture. But my dad—what was he thinking? Why would he do this? It doesn't make any sense."

"That is the question, isn't it?" Evvy says.

I pull the red folder out of my bag and spread the contents on the table. "This," I say, "Mom says this was the beginning of his plan."

We lay it open on the table, nailing down the pages that want to fly in the wind. It's pages and pages of scribbles, of spiraling circles with illegible words squeezed in the lines. *Fantasy Palace. Tony. Justice.* There are maps, two maps, one of the mountains here with the road to North Adams and all the little side roads that lead to tiny villages. The other is the Las Vegas strip. Casinos with restaurants and theatres. Pawnshops. Justices of the peace. Phone numbers. Addresses. Doodles in the margins. More scribbles.

"This makes, like, no sense." Evvy turns a page one way and then another.

I point to one of the scribbles. "No. Wait. See? Mom said that my dad was a manager for this place, Fantasy Island. And this—this FI—and the detective said there were like eight calls to Las Vegas."

"Oh, yeah. And here's another FI." Evvy shows me her page. "None of which tells us anything about where they are. Unless he's taking Adrian to Las Vegas."

"That's what I asked Mom. She says he can't get very far on forty dollars, and really what he wants to do is go to some cabin in Quebec. Hide out there. I think he wants his old job back. At the museum, or anywhere, really, but no one will hire him cause he's crazy and unreliable." I turn the blue page over in my hands, sideways and upside down, fumbling for some clue in that crazy brain. There has to be something in these stupid pages. It was my dream.

Evvy puts her hand on the page, bringing me back to the hills. "You can't go to Quebec. You just got here!"

"I know. Mom promised me she wouldn't move again, but that doesn't mean much. Promises come and go in my house." I look at the map of the mountains. It's peppered with little X's. Spots. But spots of what? "He seemed better," I say, my fingers tracing the little roads and the spots. "These last few weeks. Happy. You know, whistling and stuff. Even his doctor said he was doing better. Said that things seemed promising, that he hadn't bounced out of the depression too quickly. And that meant the meds were probably in his system and working. He was even sleeping. You know. He wasn't staying up all night, pacing the floors. Still, I think he needs to prove something to somebody."

"Or maybe he needs to remember that he is a free spirit. That this condition that holds him so tightly isn't in charge. It must be terrible to have to live with so much depression all the time. Painful. Like a Damocles that hangs from the ceiling, ready to drop. You really should try to love him, Teddy. He is your dad."

"I know. You're probably right." I straighten out the blue papers. I never should have come here. I never should have brought Evvy. I knew she would find a way to make me feel bad. "But why would he take Adrian?" I ask. "If he wanted to be free, why didn't he just go?"

"That's a good question."

The sun slides down the sky toward the west. A hawk circles overhead, wide arcs of flight.

"'Turning and turning in the widening gyre / The falcon cannot hear the falconer. / Mere anarchy is loosed upon the world.'"

"You're quoting it wrong," Evvy says.

"You get the idea. I'm like Yeats's falcon—a lost soul looking for her brother."

"Yeah. We should go. It's getting late. My mom will be worried about me." Evvy throws our napkins and plates and cups into the trash bin. One last pat on the goat's head. One last look over the horizon. I crawl in behind the wheel, more relaxed now, and we slide to the foot of the driveway and out to the road.

"Which way do we go?" I ask.

We look both ways. Neither one looks familiar. Finally, I take a left, and we head up the road.

"I really thought it would be different this time," I say.

"It is," Evvy says. "He kidnapped your little brother."

CHAPTER 18

———— ⚇ ————

A LOST SOUL IN SEARCH
OF HER BROTHER

"Evvy? Can you wake up?"

She's been sleeping since we got in the car.

"What?" She opens her eyes and flips open her phone. Still no service. "Where are we?"

"I think we're lost," I say after what seems like endless miles down the road. "No matter which way I go, it all seems wrong. So I turn around and drive some more, but we're still going the wrong way. I know that the dairy is just a few miles out of town, but I swear I drove for twenty miles one way, then twenty miles the other way, and we are totally lost."

"It's getting dark," she says. "What time is it?"

"Almost four. We still have about an hour of light."

"My mom will be worried sick about me."

"I know. Mine too," I say, although I wonder if she will.

"Is there a gas station around here where we can get directions?"

"No. Nothing."

"Did you try going back to the dairy?"

"Yes. It's gone."

"Gone? What do you mean *gone*? Teddy. You're not making any sense."

"I know. But I'm telling you, it's gone!"

Evvy is wide awake now. She grips the handle of the car door like she's going to leap out at any second. "Maybe you should turn around."

"I tried that."

"Well, try it again! Teddy! I have to get home!"

"OK. OK. Sorry." I find a shoulder and pull off, looking all ways, and then I turn around. "The wind is kicking up. Can you feel it?" I grip the wheel to hold the car steady.

Evvy crosses her arms over her chest and mutters under her breath, "None of this looks familiar."

"I know."

"The dairy was ten minutes out of town. How could you have gotten so lost?"

"I don't know!"

Damn. This isn't the right way either.

And then, out of nowhere, Arpeggio starts in with an earsplitting bark followed by an ancient howl, finally throwing himself against the back door and clawing at the window.

"Arpeggio. What?" I stop the car. Then—up there. On that hill. Under those trees. "Evvy! Look!"

I swerve onto a narrow, gravel driveway under a canopy of ancient trees. The car rumbles about fifty feet up a steep hill and stops. Up

there, perched on a hillside, there's a little red cottage. Just so. With
one window on each side of the door and a view of the enormous sky
and mountains. A kerosene lamp flickers in the windows. Smoke rises
from the small chimney. A bench sits at the foot of the three steps that
lead to the door. Everything about it is welcoming and terrifying, as if
it were drawn by a child in kindergarten. But more than any of that—

"Look, Teddy! Isn't that your dad's car?"

I shake my head. "This is so wild." Right in front of us. Dad's old,
red, rusted Mustang, the top still down, the car soaked with piles of
snow and melting snow.

Evvy looks at me, and I look at her, and I think we have stumbled
into a weird dream. But there it is, large as life.

Evvy shakes her head. "It's a hunter's lodge. Like what Mr.
Peterson told us about."

"Maybe," I say, "but where did it come from? I've been up and
down this road a dozen times, and I swear to you, it has not been
here."

"Well, it's here now," Evvy says.

The wind whistles. Crows squawk in the trees. Up in the woods,
a coyote howls. Nothing in this wild world wants us to be here.

"Do you want to go in?" I ask.

"Rescue Adrian, you mean?"

"I do."

Evvy stares at the little house. "I think I dreamt about this house
last night. Was it just last night?" She laughs. "It seems like a month
ago now. At first I thought I was home, because it's just like my old
house in Georgia," she says, "right down to the red paint, the two
windows, and the flickering yellow light of the kerosene lamp."

"Me too," I say, and we look at each other. "But this house—my house, it had all these long, dark passageways and trapdoors. It's what led me to Dad's plans."

She shakes her head. "Teddy? That house. The one in my dream. It was very scary."

I stare at the house, at the innocence of a childhood drawing in front of us, and wonder if we were in the same dream. "Is that a yes?"

"Yes, do I want to go in there?" Evvy opens her phone. Still no service. "No, I do not. But yes, do I want to rescue Adrian and take him home where he can be warm and safe? Yes." We look at each other now, the first time in what has felt like hours. She reaches out, and I take her hand. "Super quick? In and out?"

"One hundred percent," I say. "The quicker the better." But I don't move. Evvy opens her door, pushing it against the wind, and slides out. She whistles for Arpeggio, and he hops into the front seat, sniffing the air and the wind.

"Go on, puppy. Get out."

He steps out of the car, lingering back, moving quietly through the oncoming shadows.

"He doesn't like it here," Evvy says.

I step out, too, the wind gusting in the trees. "No, he doesn't. But we're here."

Arpeggio finds a tree, sniffs the roots, and marks it, a warning to the coyotes and wolves and bears that he is here, a strong, brave dog.

"Shall we go?" I point to the small cabin. One of the windows is boarded up, but the other one has a curtain. It flutters.

"What kind of strange and mystical world have we landed onto tonight?" Evvy asks.

We start up the hill. Arpeggio is right behind us. I put my hand on the small of Evvy's back. Her warmth ripples through my palm and up my arm. Neither one of us speaks. We could be walking into anything.

Dad opens the door, and the warm air from inside fills the space around us. "So." He grins. "You found us. Welcome."

"Hi, Dad." If it weren't for his low, gravelly voice, I'm not sure I would recognize him. He's wearing a faded red bathrobe over his clothes, which are both wrinkled and dirty. He hasn't shaved, his hair is wild, and his eyes are like fire. I take a deep breath. "Is Adrian here?"

"Of course he is. He's inside. He's fine." Suddenly he occupies the entire doorway, his dark shadow looming over us. I step forward, but he shifts, blocking my way. "Aren't you glad to see me?"

"I want to see my brother," I say.

"There is nothing to see," he says. "Adrian's fine. Why don't you run along. Your mother will want you to be home for supper."

We are in a showdown, a battle of wills, a third-grade staring contest where one of us will finally have to blink. He stares at me, and I stare at him, and the crows in the trees go quiet.

"Mr. Carson?" Evvy asks, and the silence collapses. "It is nice to see you, sir. We've been worried about you. Is everything all right here?"

"Yes. Thank you." He doesn't take his eyes off me, but, there, just then: he tilts his head, waiting for me to say something. That is what we call a blink.

I am supposed to blink back? To make nice? To say something like how glad I am to see him or how I have been worried sick about him or how Mom will be so pleased? But I don't mean any of it. I step forward.

He steps back.

"We're taking Adrian home. Now." My eyes are piercing.

"Teddy?" A voice from way in the back of the cabin squeaks. "Is that you?"

"Be my guest." Dad steps aside.

Arpeggio bounds into the cottage and runs to a small cot in the corner, leaping up and licking Adrian's face. Adrian is there. His bony knees are tucked up to his chest, and his skinny little arms are wrapped around his legs. "Arpeggio!"

"Adrian!" I run to him. I am going to scoop him up into my arms, but he squeals at my touch, so I back away, sitting instead at the foot of the cot. I touch his knee, but he shrivels away. Behind me, a fire smolders in the fireplace, giving Adrian's face a warm red glow and making everything warm.

"Adrian?" Evvy steps in close and kneels on the floor. Arpeggio hops down and kisses Evvy and then hops back up on the cot and kisses Adrian again. "It's me. Evvy. Sweetie? Are you OK?"

Adrian unfolds enough to wrap his arms around Arpeggio, and he bursts into tears, his face buried in the dog's fur. "I'm so sorry, Teddy," Adrian says at last. "He made me do it. He made me do everything."

"What are you talking about?"

"The magic. Bringing you here."

"No, little buddy. It's all right. No. Don't think like that. We've been looking for you. Everything's going to be all right. Evvy and Arpeggio and I are here. We're going to take you home. You're going to be all right."

But Adrian doesn't move. He reaches out and takes my hand, pulling me close, and says under his breath, "He said I had to be a man."

"Oh, Adrian."

"I tried to kill him."

The fire crackles and spits. Dad stands tall in the doorway.

"He made me shoot a gun. 'Listen. Point. Shoot,' he said."

"Come on, little buddy. It's time to go. Can you walk?"

He nods his head yes, but when he stands, he wobbles.

I wrap my arms around his waist. Evvy squeezes in on the other side of him, and on the count of three, we all stand up. Adrian wobbles in our arms, but we take a step, and then another, and lead him to the door.

"I pointed the gun right at him, but I couldn't do it. I wanted to. With all my heart I wanted to."

"It's OK, Adrian. It's all OK. We have Mom's car. Nothing else can happen now."

We stumble through the room, past an overstuffed chair, past a wooden table with five chairs, past blue papers with scribbles strewn across the table, and still more papers with still more scribbles scattered on the floor. The door is within reach.

Evvy gets there ahead of me. "Excuse me, please," she says, and Dad steps aside, not very much, just enough that she can get ahold of the doorjamb.

I step in behind, steadying Adrian with two hands on his waist, and we put one foot in front of the other. The wind is really blowing now, and the car seems like a million miles away, but, "Nice and easy. Walk. That's good." Dad steps aside, letting us pass.

It has been five long, crazy days up here in this cabin with Dad trying to turn a blind boy into a man. I can only imagine how awful it has been.

"Mom's car is just down there. Everything's going to be fine. We should be home in time for supper. Mom will be so happy to see you."

We trudge down the gravel path of the hill. Adrian is a champ.

The wind pushes against us, blowing dust and grit in our eyes, but we keep moving. Step. Step. Dad steps out behind us. He opens his arms to the heavens and lets loose a tremendous howl. He howls to the gods, and now, a mighty gust like a tornado blows up from the west, cascading down the mountains. A tree branch cracks at its trunk, splitting in two.

And then everything goes quiet.

CHAPTER 19

NATURAL OR SUPERNATURAL?

"Teddy?" Adrian asks. "What happened?"

"I have no idea."

"I heard something crack."

"I did too." I shift Adrian's weight over to Evvy. "Stay here. I'm going to investigate. Come, Arpeggio. You're with me." The dog clings to my knee, panting and whining as we wind our way to the car.

And there it is. The severed tree branch, inches from Mom's car, blocking the driveway. Amazingly, the car is fine. It barely has a scratch on it. But the road, the narrow, one-lane, gravel thing that is supposed to pass for a driveway, is completely blocked. It was an old tree, an oak, easily two feet in diameter, and the branch that fell was dead, ready to go. But I still can't believe it. Just like that, like a snap of gum, it cracked and crashed across the narrow passage, taking three smaller birch trees with it.

"It was the wind," I say when I get back to my friends. "The wind hit that old oak tree, splitting it in two, and now it's blocking the car."

Adrian lifts his nose to the wind. "It wasn't the wind. It was Dad. We're trapped."

"Dad? You think he lifts his arms and yells something, and suddenly an old, dead branch breaks? That's absurd."

"No. Really. I'm telling you. I've been here. I know."

The longer I look at the car, the tree, the gravel driveway, the endless horizon beyond, the less anything makes any sense. I see it, but I don't see it, and Adrian sags in my arms, his weight becoming unbearable.

Dad claps his hands and parades toward us, his red bathrobe billowing behind him. "Wow. That was some wind, huh?" He has this big, ugly grin on his small, ugly face. "Come on in, kids. Nothing to do now but make a good, hearty supper."

The wind whistles. Dust and sand swirl around us, getting in my eyes.

"I can't go back in there," Adrian pleads, and for a minute, a full minute, none of us moves. We stand at the center of this wind storm with the broken tree branch on one side of us and the cabin on the other.

"I don't think we have a choice," I say. "I'm sorry, Adrian. We'll think of something. I promise." And the four of us, the old gang of four—me, Evvy, Adrian, and Arpeggio—climb the hill through this forest in silence. The woods are coming alive with the advent of night, and everywhere, it seems, leaves rustle with hungry, waking animals.

We don't talk. My heart throbs in my chest, and I can barely put one foot in front of the other. The sun is completely buried by the horizon now, and the first sign of the moon creeps up through the trees. The temperature starts to plummet. And now Evvy, who once kissed me under the Guider Tree and promised to love me forever, who once helped me shovel a foot of snow from the driveway, and who even called me the bomb, now she is going to get a chance to see my dad, up close and personal. This is not going to be pretty.

The door creaks open, and warm air surrounds us.

Dad is on his knees in front of the fireplace. An oil lamp flickers on a low table beside him, and large shadows dance around the cabin. A pile of logs sits next to old newspaper and kindling. "Welcome!" He sits back on his heels. "You ever been in a hunter's lodge? This is a hunter's lodge." He's all smiles. "Folks 'round here, they keep it stocked so's they have somewhere to go after a long day of shooting animals. Look in the kitchen. There's pasta and lots of canned food. You should be able to cook up a wonderful meal for us. I'll bet you're all pretty hungry."

"Dad?" I ask. "How long have you been planning this?"

"Oh." For a moment, a flash of an instant, guilt sweeps over his face. "Planning? Sweetheart. What are you talking about?"

"I'm talking about this, Dad. This thing with Adrian, this game you're playing. Because it's not fun."

"Now, sweetie. There's no cause to be upset. I used to drive these hills, you know, for work, and these lodges, they're scattered all over these mountains. Wonderful places. Completely off the grid. You're going to love it here."

"No, Dad. We want to go home."

Adrian crawls back into his corner on the cot, squeezing his knees and wrapping his arms. Evvy stands behind me. She's looking around, probably, hopefully, for some kind of escape hatch.

"And, oh. Well. Gosh. Let me see." He puts a log onto the embers and pushes the fire around. It crackles and sends embers into the room, and his face glows with the hot pink light. "Not sure there's much I can do 'bout that. Not till morning anyway. That old tree branch, you know. But there's a loft. Just up there." He points to a ladder ascending into the ceiling. "Yup. Sleeping bags and everything. Adrian's been on the cot down here with me, but hell—plenty of room up there for the three of you. I can sleep on this little cot. Be nice to stretch out. We'll be fine here to ride out the storm."

"Storm? What storm?"

Dad winks, a glint in his eye, and lightning flashes across the sky. I count, "One Mississippi ... two Mississippi ... three Mississ—" and then a crack of thunder echoes off the mountains. It sounds like gunfire. I wonder if the animals up here ever get used to it. Dad strikes another match.

The wind howls, and smoke pours into the cabin.

"Dad! Wait! Did you open the flue to the chimney?"

The match goes out. He lights another. "Of course I did, Teddy. Relax. You're so jumpy. Adrian and me, we've been here for days. I know what I'm doing." He shuffles the paper and the logs, making them just right, and a second flame catches on the paper. The fireplace is littered with dead matches. He stands up, brushing his knees. "That should do it. The embers are still pretty hot."

I stand there, paralyzed like a total dope with nothing to say. Evvy pushes past me and my dad and sits with Adrian on the cot. She puts her hand on his knee. He starts to rock back and forth, humming, flapping his fingers in front of his face. I've never seen him like this. Arpeggio hops on the cot with them, wriggling in between them and leaning on Adrian's knee. He stops rocking and scratches the dog behind his ear.

"Deep breaths, Adrian," Evvy whispers.

They are a perfect still life.

"There are some warm clothes in that trunk over there," Dad says, a big smile stretching across his face. "Jeans and sweats. That sort of thing. Get out of those city clothes. You'll freeze in them."

And then he sits. At the table. And takes one of his scribbled pages and begins to work. To do something with it, turning it one way and then another, making notes with his pencil. "It's nice to see you, Teddy. I'm glad you came."

I smile back, but I don't mean it. I walk past him, my head high, gritting my teeth and ignoring him the best I can. I rifle through the trunk and find some warm pajamas for Evvy and a flannel bathrobe for Adrian—blue and faded—and what looks like clean underwear. I find another pair of sweats and a sweatshirt for me. They smell clean and fresh, like they've been hanging on a clothesline with a gentle pine scent wafting through the air. I hold up a towel so Evvy can have some privacy to change, but I see her peeking around the edge to check out my dad. We drape our towels over the chairs and fold our clothes neatly into a pile. Evvy and Adrian huddle together by the fire.

She whispers in my ear, "Adrian says there is a bad spirit near here."

I whisper back. "Near here? Or in here?"

Evvy nods. "Near here. That's what he says."

"Ha! He's good, that kid," Dad says, his words bouncing off every wall. "You know he says he's a ghost whisperer?"

"I know, Dad. He can feel things."

"Yup. And he is so very, very right. Something big is headed our way." And he laughs again. "You're going to love it."

Evvy ignores him. "Someone, Adrian. What did you say?"

"Guilt and shame. Guilt and shame." He starts to rock and flap his hands again. "Closer. Closer."

I kneel beside the cot, taking Adrian's hand in mine. I squeeze it and shake my head. Mom? Crystal Falls? Mr. Harrison? These things seem so very far away now, specks on a past that I don't remember. I put Arpeggio's paw in the fold with me and Adrian. Evvy puts her hand in too. Arpeggio and I rub noses, and for this nanosecond, things seem normal. He wags his little tail and licks my nose.

Evvy speaks softly, so only we can hear: "At this point, nothing would surprise me."

"Natural or supernatural. Do you know the difference?" I imitate Mr. Harrison, writing the words up on the board. "Yup. Pretty soon, we should hear Ariel on his flute. Maybe she can help us move that tree that landed in front of our car. Get us the hell out of this log scene."

Arpeggio curls up beside Adrian, giving his weight and his comfort. Quiet settles over the cabin. Adrian relaxes, tumbling into a soft pile of fresh clothes and tender dreams. I stare at the fire, watching sparks crackle and embers shift from red to orange to yellow. Outside, a fierce wind whistles through the trees. When my face is hot and my stomach rumbles, I whisper to Evvy, "You hungry?"

She nods.

Dad is right about one thing. This place is ready for company. There's a propane stove and a well-stocked kitchen. Food and warm beer. There's even a sink with an old-fashioned pump for well water. I find a pot and put some water on the stove for rice. There is some canned corn and a few tins of chicken. Two tuna cans are empty, piled into the trash bin in the corner. A third sits on the counter. Next to the trash, there is a wooden box with some old carrots. Yeah. I can make something for us. Even Arpeggio can do with some chicken and rice. At least it's something.

I open a warm beer and pour it into a glass.

"What are you doing?" Evvy asks.

"Having something to drink. You want some?"

She shakes her head, in disgust, I'm sure, for all my decadent ways, but she finds a glass and pours some for herself. We lift our glasses and take a sip. Then another. She tries her phone again. Still no service. "My mom is going to flip out." She pulls the map out of her bag and lays it out on the table in front of my dad. "Maybe you can tell us where we are, Mr. Carson."

He looks at the map and then at Evvy. I hold my breath, waiting for what he will do when he sees the map that was in the red folder in the box in the back of the basement, and how did she get it?

"Did I ever tell you the story of when Teddy was in kindergarten and she and her best friend—"

"Nobody cares, Dad," I say, but he babbles on anyway about the time my mom said I could do a sleepover at my best friend's house, and I was so excited that I started shadowboxing in the front hall and put my arm through the window. "Harriet wrapped her arm in a thousand rags and whisked her off to the hospital for stitches. And then," he says, laughing, "she went back to the hospital the next day, saying, 'Those were my best rags.'"

Even Evvy laughs.

Adrian weaves his way through the cabin, circling his way around Dad at the table.

"Teddy?" he asks, curling his body into mine. "Do you know what happened? Do you know why are we here?"

I put my arm around his shoulder. "Good question. I have no idea, but for some reason, Dad brought you up here. On an adventure, I think. But then Evvy and I, we didn't know what happened. We were worried about you, so we came looking for you. And we found you. Isn't that great? Now, we're all going to have something to eat, and then we'll figure something out, how to get out of here. We might be stuck here till morning, though, I'm afraid."

"Teddy?"

"Yes, little buddy?"

"You do believe me, don't you? About Dad, I mean. That he wanted you to come."

"Oh, gosh. I ... I don't know. Nothing makes sense, so maybe. Why not?" I try to laugh it off, but Adrian doesn't even crack a smile. "You think the tree was him too?"

"I do."

"Oh, Adrian. What is happening to you?" I put my arms around him and hold him close. His body trembles next to mine, but his breath is deep, and his heart is strong. Neither one of us wants to let go, so we stand in the kitchen while the wind rides in wide circles through the treetops and the rain patters on the roof.

Adrian wriggles out. "Teddy? Tell me what this place looks like."

"You haven't explored it?"

"A little, but mostly I stumble over things."

I take his cheeks in my hands and kiss him on the forehead. The sky lights up, and I count. It's many Mississippi's till the thunder comes again, just wind and rain and more rain.

While the water boils, I put the pasta in, and we take a grand tour. "Well, from the outside, it looks like a house you would draw in kindergarten, with a door in the middle and two windows, a chimney with smoke, and a little bench to one side. Welcoming, you know. But inside, it's a square room. A rectangle really, more wide than long." I take his hands and stretch them wide. "This is the kitchen area. It has a sink with a pump for water." I rest one of his hands on the pump and the other under the water. He pumps some water and laughs, his whole body jiggling.

"And over here, where Dad is sitting—hi, Dad—there's a table with five chairs. Isn't that odd? Five chairs. Not four. But five. And over here, on the way to the fireplace … here. Can you feel the rug on the floor?"

"I can. It's braided, right?"

"Right. It's pretty old, I think, with blue and red and what was probably white strips of fabric braided together. It's between the kitchen area and the fireplace. And here"—I put his hand on a big chair—"this is an easy chair. What's it covered with?"

"It feels like a blanket."

"Exactly. The chair is corduroy, dark brown, but faded and stained, so now it's covered with a blanket. One of those crochet things. Yellow and orange. You remember your colors?"

"Not really."

I lean over and whisper in his ear, "It's pretty ugly."

Adrian laughs.

"There's a loft area up above." Dad points. "The ladder's over there. See the ladder?"

"I see it, Dad. But, I'm sorry. Where is the bathroom?"

He laughs, a good, strong belly laugh, filling the whole cabin with his sour breath. "It's outside. Around to the side. There's a moon and a star on the door. You can't miss it."

"In the rain?"

"Yup. Wait." Dad rifles through the trunk that had the clothes. It's still packed with blankets and pillows. "Man against the elements!" he says. "What did my teacher call it in history? Lo those many years ago when I was in high school? Ah yes. High school. Those were great days. Right! Rugged individualism. The American dream. Manifest Destiny. That's what this country was built on. Courage. Right, Adrian? Good, old-fashioned, manly courage." He throws some sleeping bags at Evvy, nearly knocking her over. "Take these upstairs to the loft. There are some up there, but these can be extras. In case you get cold." He mutters under his breath, "I was sure I saw it in here."

Look at him: his nose in the trunk, his soul in fool's paradise, blankets up to his knees strewn across the floor. The kerosene lamp flickers on the table, sending enormous shadows dancing across the walls. His has the face of an ox, long and drawn, and even though he is laughing, his shadow is not. I'm not sure which one is real.

Outside, the moon is trapped by the clouds, and the night air is thick with rain. It looks like it's going to go on for a while. I put out plates and glasses and a bowl for Arpeggio. I fill his bowl with rice and some chicken.

"Found it!" Dad bellows, and he pulls out a porcelain bowl. "A bathroom. Right here. It's the way people used to pee at night. Me and Adrian, we've been standing in the doorway and letting her whizz. Ain't that right, Adrian? But this is how folks used to do it. I mean way back in the day. Like in Shakespeare's times. We'll put it … um …" He walks around the cabin looking for a private spot, but there isn't one, so he puts it in the corner of the kitchen. On one of the chairs. "Here. Yes. Here. This is good, isn't it, kids? Now, isn't this romantic? Up in the mountains, a rain storm, a cabin with everything we might need. What could be cooler than this?" He grins. "Ah! This is such stuff as dreams are made on. That's Shakespeare, you know. From *The Twelfth Night*, I think. Have you read Shakespeare yet?"

"Yes, Dad. And it's from *The Tempest*."

"Well, aren't you smart? You're in high school, right?"

He takes this weird stance where he opens his chest wide, thumps his foot, leans back, and claps. "Oh, come on. You're here now. Nothing you can do about anything, so try to enjoy it." But none of us say anything. "Come on, kids. Nothing to be afraid of. It's a hunting lodge."

"Come on, Arpeggio. Let's you and I step outside and pee," Evvy says, and she opens the door. It's a steady rain now. The thunder has moved on to another hill. Lightning flashes in the distance. Arpeggio stands in the doorway and looks back at me. I nod, and he steps out.

"Did he go out?" Adrian asks.

"Yes. He did."

"He's amazing," Adrian says. "He's as scared as we are, but he is going to be brave for you."

Dad babbles all through dinner, which is not bad, if I do say so myself. He doesn't taste it though. He wants to know everything about Evvy—how she learned to play piano, her art, her favorite subject, what she's reading. With every answer, he asks her three more questions, and the two of them are in it, deep in conversation, and pretty soon he's sharing folktales of the Mohican and Algonquin peoples who once ruled this whole area. "So many tribes," he says, and he's lost in his own reverie, "in scattered outposts from Greenland to Idaho to Delaware. And this one is from the Passamaquoddy Peoples of eastern Maine." He leans in, and Evvy is the only person in the world. "This is the one where Koluscap, a most revered leader of his people, turns Cihkonaqc, his lazy, good-for-nothing uncle, into a turtle. A tortoise, really. His skin might be crusty and shriveled, but 'You will have a long life. Why, you'll roll in fire, live on land and in the water, and if they cut off your head? Ha! You can live for another nine days.'"

"These are wonderful!" Evvy laughs and claps with him. "Where did you learn all this?"

"From talking with people," he says. "Just talking. Everyone has a story, you know, and life is better when you live close to literature. Isn't that right, Teddy?"

I glare at him in silence, picking up the spoon. "There's a little left. Does anyone want some more?" I ask, but no one answers. I look over at Evvy. She has her phone out. Again. There is still no service.

"And now," Dad announces, "for the piece de resistance. Some fresh, homemade cookies." He pulls out a plate of what look like chocolate chip cookies, pale and doughy, just the way I like them.

"Oh. These looks terrific. You made them?" Evvy asks.

"I did. The morning before we left. Try them. They're a little stale now, but they're delicious."

I put one in my mouth and spit it out. "Dad! What's in here?"

"Anchovies!" He laughs. "Isn't that great? No one has ever put anchovies in cookies before. It's a new recipe. I made it myself. Here. Have another."

"I'll pass, thanks."

"Evvy?" he asks.

"No thank you. But it certainly was a surprise."

I scrape my food into Arpeggio's bowl, and he devours everything, leaving only a small heap of anchovies in the corner.

"You don't want those?" I ask. He doesn't. I open the door and fling the salty, dead fish into the wind.

"God, Teddy. You've told me such hideous, awful stories about your dad, but he's really amazing." Evvy clears the table, and we stand together at the sink. "He knows so much about this area." She hums a tune.

I try to hum with her, but I can't. How many times have I heard this? How lucky I am to have him for a dad. When they meet my family, they either tell me I'm exaggerating or they run. There's no middle ground with my dad, no earth on which he can plant a tree and let it take root.

The fire fades into ashes. I hand her a plate to dry, but there is nothing to say. Dad shuffles around the cabin, looking for something. He looks in the wood box, under the cot, in the cabinets behind my knees. Finally, he lights a second kerosene lamp, and the room fills with a soft yellow light. The shadows shrink. He whistles and thumps out a tune with his fingers, checking the sound of every surface in the cabin, filling the place with a claustrophobic noise.

"Any idea what time it is?" she asks.

"None. Ten maybe? Eleven?"

"I was hoping when the storm passed that we could get some service. Even a bar so I could text my mom. She must be out of her mind. I've never been gone like this."

"I know. Maybe she called Detective Malloy. Maybe he's out looking for us right now."

Adrian gropes his way through the room and stands next to me. He wraps his arm around my waist. "I'm scared, Teddy."

"I know, little buddy. We all are. But let's not think about that."

"Tell us," Evvy says, "about the spirit. The one you thought was here."

"Don't listen to him!" Dad yells. Even though we whisper, our voices carry across the cabin, bouncing off the walls like the crackling of the fire. Dad throws another log onto the fire, damp pinewood, and it spits hot embers into the room. "Adrian? I mean it."

"Yes, Dad." Adrian folds, almost in two, and limps back toward the cot.

"Ignore him." Evvy leaps in front of Adrian, his shoulders in her hands. She guides him back to the kitchen. "It's fine. It's all fine. Tell us what happened."

"But what about Dad?" he asks.

"Teddy and I are here. We're right here. Nothing's going to happen. Is it, Mr. Carson?"

Dad grumbles, pushing fresh logs around. Flames catch and spread. He stands up, brushing the ashes from his knees. He says nothing. Adrian turns to us. He speaks so softly I can barely hear him, and I'm three inches away. "The first time I felt it was like"—he counts on his fingers—"three days ago. It was a cold shadow. It blew through. At first I thought it was a draft through the window, but then I heard it. The whistle. Something is going to happen."

"A whistle? Like a flute?" I ask. "Maybe Ariel was here."

"Don't be ridiculous," Evvy snaps at me.

"Hey," I snap right back at her. "Sorry. It was supposed to be a joke."

"More like the kind you make when you blow on a blade of grass." Adrian lifts his face, tilting his head to catch something with his ears. He shifts around the table and gropes his way toward the fireplace. Dad is back at the table, spreading out his papers and thrumming his fingers. Adrian turns back to us. "But I'm sorry, Teddy. I don't hear it now."

"That's fine," I say.

Evvy glares at me and follows Adrian to the cot. She takes his hands in hers. "And this one may be too hard, but try," Evvy says. "How long has that spirit been wandering around near here?"

"Oh, wow." Adrian laughs. "I've never thought about that. Time is always so fluid in the spirit world. But it was a cold wind. It started soon after we got here."

Even with the warmth of the fire filling every crevice of the cabin, a chill runs up my spine.

CHAPTER 20

MORE TWISTING AND WINDING

"Come on now. Time for bed. All of you. Hip hop. Big day tomorrow, so the sandman's coming."

His moods are flipping so fast now. He's shuffling his emotional cards, and everything is whirring, and I don't know what Dad I'm looking at, but he draws a card—and whoosh! Good mood!

"Dad?" I ask. "What is tomorrow?"

"You'll see." His face fills with an ugly grin.

"What the hell does that mean?"

"Teddy?" He flaps a finger my way. "Your language. Please."

"No, Dad!" I insist. "Tell us."

Whoosh! Power mood. Dad doesn't say anything. He just folds his arms and keeps on grinning.

"It's OK, Teddy." Evvy touches my shoulder. "Let's figure this loft out."

Evvy takes Adrian by the elbow and leads him toward the ladder. "Come on, Adrian. Let's check out this loft."

"Not you, Adrian. You come with me."

"But, Dad—it's still raining."

"'But, Dad?' Is that what you said to me? 'But, Dad?' Your sister and her little friend may be here, but nothing changes. You hear me? Nothing!"

Adrian curls his knees into his chest and wraps his arms. He rocks back and forth.

"Now, Adrian!" Dad stretches his rubbers over his shoes. "And don't act so lazy. I'll turn you into a tortoise." Ooh. Icky grin. "Come. Door."

With one last moan, Adrian unfurls and lifts himself from the cot. He reaches for the chair, but it is too far. In three long strides, I reach Adrian and wrap my arm around his waist, helping him walk to the door. "It's OK, Adrian. Me and Evvy. We're right here."

Dad looks around the cabin. He looks again. "Adrian? Where's the rifle?"

"I ... I put it in the corner by the trunk."

"It's not there."

"Are you sure?"

"I'm looking right at it. There is no rifle in the corner." Dad searches the corner, pulling everything out of the trunk, throwing it back in, pulling it out again, and shoving the whole trunk into the room with a screech. The lid crashes down. No rifle. "It can't have just disappeared. What did you do with it, Adrian?"

"Nothing, Dad. I swear. Can we do this tonight without it? Please?"

Dad takes one last look and shakes his head. "Fine." He opens the door, and Adrian shuffles behind him. "I knew this would happen," Dad mutters. "I teach you some magic, and you use it against me."

The two of them step outside into the last of the rain. There is some humming.

"This place gets weirder by the minute." Evvy shivers and points to the door. "What do you think they're doing?"

We creep to the door, laying our ears against it to listen. It is impossible to know what we are hearing. It's humming in two-part harmony, and the melody, if that's what you can call it, twists and winds in circles that get pretty loud. It sounds like cicadas in the trees, and then it stops. It goes quiet, and rain patters on the roof. Then the humming starts up again, with more twisting and more winding. For five full minutes, Adrian and Dad repeat this ritual. Arpeggio sits at the door with us and howls his small dog howls.

"Shh, puppy." I put my finger on my lips, and he goes quiet. He still howls, but it is soft, something he keeps tucked in his lips.

And then it goes quiet again.

Until a squeaky whoop rings out, peeling and echoing off the mountains, followed by a loud clapping and Dad's creepy laugh. "That's my man! Yup." More clapping. "Good job, Adrian!" Even though Dad's voice is muffled by the door and the rain, his excitement rings through. "Come on, old chap. Let's get you dried off."

We dash across the room, and I whistle for Arpeggio just as the door swings open, the screen door slaps, and Dad steps in, dripping with rain. Evvy scrambles up the ladder. Smart woman.

"I thought you were in the loft."

My heart throbs in my ears.

"I ... I mean we ... Dad. Please. I only came back down to get ... um ... Arpeggio. Come on, puppy." Arpeggio sits at Adrian's feet, staring up into his eyes. "Puppy. Come. You, too, Adrian."

"Adrian?" Dad scowls. Adrian stands, his back stiff against Dad's voice. "I've changed my mind. You're a man now. The men can sleep down here."

I've known my dad all my life, and he's been off the wall more than once, but this. This! This humming and the rain and the red bathrobe and the paper with scribbles and—hell—even his being here! This I don't understand. This scares me.

Adrian shakes his head. "I ... I want to stay with Teddy," he stammers.

"What did you say, Tortoise? Speak up!"

"I ... I want to stay with Teddy," he says again, a little louder.

Dad looks at Adrian, then at me. "That's better. Talk like a man. Stand up straight. Take your ridiculous hands out of your pockets and talk to me like you mean it." He grumbles something else that I cannot hear and throws his jacket across the room. "When you're a man, you can do what you like."

"Yes, sir."

"That's more like it. Up you go. Go hide behind the girls."

I grab a towel. "Come on, Adrian," I whisper. "Let's check out this loft, shall we?" I lead him across an endless, treacherous terrain of discarded paper and chairs splayed in all directions. "Put your hands here, little buddy." I try to sound calm. "And step up. That's it. Hand over hand. I have a towel and some dry clothes. We'll dry you off." Adrian goes first as rung by rung we climb, ascending into a dark hole. The loft space is four, maybe four and a half feet high, and there is a peak at the top of the ceiling with rafters. There's just enough room to crawl on all fours, barely enough to sit up. There are three sleeping bags wedged up against the walls and a small, round window on the far wall over here, by the ladder. Outside, the storm starts to move on, and a little spit of full moon drifts in and out behind the clouds. I grope my way toward the back, helping Adrian find his way.

At least it's dry. Are there rats up here? Do they even come up this high?

I crawl back down the ladder, sling my book bag over my shoulder, and pick up Arpeggio. "Come on, puppy. You're with us." I clutch him close to my chest, balance him in one arm—all forty-something pounds of him—and reach for the rung with the other. I lift us both up and find a spot for my foot. Arpeggio doesn't like this idea at all. No. Not one little bit, and he whines in my ear and wriggles and squirms, and it's all I can do to hold him with one hand and the ladder with the other, but I do. I let go of the ladder and reach for the rung and find it with my foot and pull. I plant my second foot and kiss him on the cheek. "Two down. Six to go."

But before I can get up to the third rung, he has clawed his way out of my arms and landed on the floor. "Ow! That was my neck!" He lies down and puts his chin on his front paws, wagging his tail and looking at me with those liquid black eyes of his. "What? You want to stay down here?" I ask. "With Dad? Because I'm going up there. You can come with me or stay here. Your choice."

He looks at Dad, who is back at the table, the oil lamp flickering. More paper. More scribbles. Then he looks at me and sits up, just as tall and straight as a good puppy can.

"That's better."

I wrap him in a towel and pick him up again. "Try to trust me." I rub his head and whisper in his ear, "I know I've been wrong about everything today, but please ..." And once again, we climb, him in one arm, me grabbing the ladder rails with the other. When I get to the top rung, he scrambles out of my arms and curls up beside Adrian, staring at me. Even in the dark, with a creepy moon drifting in and out behind the thinning clouds, I can feel his intensity.

"Yeah, OK. I get it. You're pissed. You don't want to be here. I don't like it either, but we're here. And we're alive. At least I think we're alive. Unless we really have landed in hell."

Evvy hands me a towel, and I dry Adrian's hair. From her hands shines a light.

"A flashlight! You're so smart."

"I found it by the stove. This place does have everything." She crawls toward the second sleeping bag and nestles into the corner, the light from the flashlight skirting over the cobwebs and rafters.

Adrian messes with his sleeping bag, pushing it in every direction. "Teddy? Why can't Dad just love us? I mean just the way we are?"

"I don't know, little buddy," and of all the things in the last days that I don't know, this has to be the biggest one yet. "I wish I knew."

"I want to go home."

"I know. We all do."

I dry him off with the towel, stripping his wet clothes off and tossing them into a heap by the window. Evvy shines the flashlight on some red reindeer pajama bottoms and a black T-shirt, and I manage to get him into the pants, one foot at a time, without banging his head on the ceiling. I rub him down till he giggles from the touch.

Adrian crawls into his bag. He grabs me by my arm and pulls me close. "I'm telling you, Teddy, you have to believe me—he brought you here, *summoned* you, but you were just practice."

"We got lost," Evvy says. "There's no magic in that."

"Maybe not," Adrian tells her. "But I'm telling you, he's waiting for someone. He's calling out to the gods every night. And because I can feel spirits, he's got me in it too. I know all that. And someone is coming, but I just don't know who."

"Is that what the humming thing is about?"

"Yeah. It's pretty creepy, isn't it? We've been doing this same creepy humming thing every night since we got here. He's obsessed. He says he can raise storms with it, get people lost and disoriented, and that he can lure them here with his humming. And then, Teddy. Then he makes me shoot the gun. 'Listen,' he says. 'Point. Shoot.' I think he's either going to turn me into a man or a tortoise. He's convinced that if I don't go hunting, I'll be a fag or something."

"Like me," I say.

"Yeah. Sort of." He laughs, but then real serious, he says, "Teddy? Did you hide the rifle?"

"Me? No. Not me. Evvy?"

"Not me either."

"Arpeggio?" Arpeggio sits, his very, very, very best dog sit, and swishes his tail. If I didn't know better, I would say he was smiling.

"This place gives me the creeps. I really, really, really want to go home."

"I know, little buddy. We'll think of something. Try to get some sleep."

"If I had had that gun tonight, I think I would have shot him. Teddy, he's my father. My dad. He raised me, and I wanted to kill him!"

Oh, Lord. I wrap my arms around my little brother and curl my body next to his, whispering over and over that we'll think of something, that somehow we'll get him out of here, we'll all be OK.

It doesn't take him long to drift off, his soft snores flopping around.

I nudge Arpeggio out of the way and slide into the other sleeping bag next to Evvy, a narrow thing jutting out into the room. It's surprisingly soft and comfortable, even though it only rests on a thin mat.

The wind blows through the treetops.

Downstairs, Dad whistles and thumps.

The fire crackles with wet logs and pine sap.

A coyote howls in the distance.

Something scratches at the door.

"Is that a bear?" I ask.

"I think it's a coyote."

More than anything, I want to pee.

"It's an orchestra of sounds," I say, "both inside and out."

"However awful this is," Evvy says, "I'm glad to be inside."

I wrap my arms around her. Arpeggio relents and nestles at our feet, his head on my ankles, his hips on her feet. We are united by the dog. "I'm so sorry, Ev. If I had known this was going to happen, I never would have …"

"I know."

Dad opens the door, and the smell of fresh rain fills the cabin. He chops wood.

"Is he OK?"

I laugh. "I don't even know what that means. Do you mean, is he OK chopping wood by the light of a kerosene lamp, or is he OK living with a mental illness?"

"Mmm. I see what you mean. I guess I mean both."

Evvy turns the flashlight on again, and I stare at the ceiling, the rough-cut wood with random pine knots and beams that stretch between one wall and the other. It's well made, this cabin. "I guess I don't know. For either one."

"Oh, Teddy." She touches my arm. "Your dad, he's charming and wonderful and scary and unpredictable, all rolled up in one. Has he always been like this?"

"No. But in the last few years, it seems like it's getting worse. He can be pretty crazy at times. Except when he's depressed. Then he disappears like a gopher down a dark hole. My mom begs him to stay on his meds, and I thought he was. We all thought he was doing better."

"Can't you get some help for him?"

I wriggle just an inch closer to her, resting my head against her heart, listening to the soft lub-dubs. "We thought we were. You know, a psychiatrist. Meds. And we've given him time. Lots of time. I really thought the meds were working. He seemed happy again. Whistling. But the law says he can't be forced to take them. That's what my mom says anyway."

Evvy runs her fingers through my hair. "You've tried a hundred times to tell me about him, and I always thought you were exaggerating. I'm sorry." She holds me tight. I try not to cry. I try my very, very best, but hot tears dribble down my cheeks. I wipe my nose on my sleeve, and Evvy laughs. And that makes me laugh, and Evvy drops her voice, just like Detective Malloy. "Now, girls—how did you say you ended up in that cabin?"

I laugh. "Well, sir. You see it was like this ..."

"And don't forget the anchovy cookies," she says, and now I laugh, a big, deep, quiet belly laugh.

"I know." She runs her hand up my arm, and my skin tingles. "We need a plan."

"Mmm." I wrap in closer to her. The rosemary in her shampoo mingles with her sweat, and I am filled with longing. I run my hand across her belly, but her skin does not tingle. "We had a plan. Look where it got us."

"Teddy?" she asks. "I have an idea. Did you bring a book with you?"

Ah. Right. A plan. I sigh and pull my hand away. "I think I have *The Tempest*. Why?"

She props up on one elbow. "Because we can close our eyes and open it to a page. Wherever we land, that will give us some insight as to what we should do."

"Really?"

"Really. Trust me."

"OK." I don't for a hot second believe her, but I fish around in my bag and drag out *The Tempest*. "Close my eyes, you say?"

"And open the page. Run your finger down. And read where you are."

"Wherever I land?"

"Yes," she says. "Read."

I clear my throat, and she focuses the flashlight on my finger. The words seem to dance across the page, but I read.

"'You taught me language, and my profit on't / Is I know how to curse.'"

She lies back down, repeating the line over and over. Finally she asks, "Whose line is that?"

I open the book and find my place. "Caliban. Act one, scene two."

"Good. OK. Read it again," she says.

And I do, dragging my tongue over the language and the profit and the curse, trying to make sense of it all. "I don't see how this helps us."

I feel the words spinning around in Evvy's head as she whispers, "I get it. Do you get it?"

"No." I laugh.

"OK. Follow me here. Mr. Harrison wanted you to audition for Ariel, right?"

"Yeah. But—"

"Ariel and Caliban are like siblings. Ariel is Prospero's good fairy. That's you. But Caliban. He's the deformed one. Adrian is the pretty one, the sprite, the fairy."

"The queer?"

"Maybe. The one who will do Prospero's bidding. But Caliban, he's the ghost whisperer, the one who knows all the secrets. Your dad steals his secrets, but he doesn't respect him. He calls him Tortoise if he doesn't move fast enough and says he's not a real man if he can't shoot a gun. And what does Caliban get for all this stuff that Prospero's doing with him?"

"He wants to kill him. Wow, yeah. Dad said to him tonight, 'I taught you some magic, and you use it against me.'"

"Whoa. That's it." Evvy lies back down, and the flashlight sweeps across the ceiling. "'You taught me language, and my profit on't / Is I know how to curse.' Poor Adrian. Your dad is trying to give him the gift of manhood, but instead he has learned to curse this man." She turns the flashlight off and cradles it on her chest. Even in this tiny space, the darkness is almost infinite. "How sad," she says.

Dad opens the door again. Whatever had been out there scratching at the door is gone. The storm floats away, and crickets sing in the wavering moonlight. An owl hoots. Whoosh. Thump. Whoosh. Thump.

"He's chopping more wood."

"Shh."

I roll in a touch closer to her and push her hair out of her face. I run my fingers down her cheek. She's been crying too. I dry her eyes.

Then I close her eyes and lean over and kiss her. She wraps her arm around me, pulling me in close, and she kisses me back, and nothing in my whole entire life has ever felt so good or so right. I know that on this dark night, in this little cabin, stranded up here in these mountains, she sees all the way through me. I am as clear as rushing river water, as deep as a deep lake, and she holds me in her arms. I am safe. I am alive. I open my eyes. I see it in her, too, and I have never loved anyone the way I love her.

Dad comes in, whistling, and drops the wood on the floor by the fireplace. It sounds like he chopped many pieces. He throws a log onto the fire. It's wet, and it crackles.

"Everything's OK," he calls up to us. "It's all under control."

As the wood dries and the sparks settle down, Evvy and Arpeggio drift toward sleep. "Maybe when we wake up in the morning," Evvy whispers, "I'll be in my bed at home, warm and safe."

"Yeah, maybe."

I lie awake for what seems like hours, trying to understand my dad. "You taught me language and my profit on't / is I know how to curse."

Maybe he tried to love us. I don't remember.

Was he always like this? When we lived in Minnesota, he would be up into the night, pacing around, snapping his fingers, thrumming a rhythm on the arm of the sofa, the back of a chair, the edge of a table. In the morning, he would be sound asleep in a chair somewhere, his head collapsed on the desk or the table in front of him, papers strewn on the floor. Nothing but scribbles. Random words. Doodles of birds and cages and rabbits.

Mom would tell us not to disturb him. She said she would wake him later, and he would go to work.

And usually, I think, he would.

So, when did it start?

I cycle around inside my head. Evvy's slow, steady breathing is beside me on one side; Adrian's soft, sloppy snores are on the other. At my feet, Arpeggio sighs and shifts, nearly crushing my feet with his love.

And then I am back on the ship, and the storm comes up out of nowhere, and we are sliding around on the deck, and the ship tips over, and we all slide into the raging water.

CHAPTER 21

UNDER THE APPLE TREE

It's that pull on my bladder that wakes me up. *Please let me be at home.*
Please let me be at home. But when I open my eyes, I am still in the
cabin. Up in the loft. The rain has stopped, and a clear morning light
cracks over the mountains. Evvy is beside me, and her soft breath is
like a simple wind in the treetops. Adrian's sleeping bag is in knots
around him. Dad is asleep, his breath snorting and grabbing for air.
I try my hardest to lie very still up here, but after a few minutes, or
maybe a half hour, or maybe a day or two, I have lost track of time
and what time even is. I slip out of the warm body loft and crawl,
putting my feet on the top rungs of the ladder. I peek downstairs.
Dad's sprawled out in the overstuffed chair. More papers are strewn
around on the floor.

"Arpeggio. Psst!"

Arpeggio lifts his head, but he doesn't move. I open my arms and
whistle for him. He glares at me, but he gets up, gives himself a good
stretch, and walks into my arms. He's tense. He does not want to look

over the edge. He backs away. *You can lead a cow up the stairs, but you cannot lead a cow down the stairs.* I never thought that information would ever, in a million years, be useful, but there it is. I have to get my dog down this ladder.

"Psst. OK, puppy. You got this." I wrap him in my arms, and despite all his attempts to wriggle out and leap back into the sleeping bag with Evvy, the two of us descend the ladder. I put the dog down, and my neck itches with his dander and anxiety.

Dad rearranges his position on the chair. "Good morning, sleepyhead."

"Don't talk to me." I open the door. "Come on, puppy. Let's go."

"Oh, sweetie. Don't be like that. Look where we are! It's paradise. I went out early this morning and picked some fresh apples off that tree out front. Try some. They're very tasty."

I whistle for Arpeggio, and the two of us step outside. Arpeggio dashes to the apple tree, sniffing every root and shave of bark. A large V of geese, maybe forty of them, fly overhead, each one honking the beginning of today's journey. I stare at them, watching them disappear to the south and wishing it could somehow be that easy to get away.

The gravel path is clear now, but I can see where it leads. I think I can even see where the car is parked and where the tree crashed in front of it. I follow Arpeggio, duck behind the apple tree, and squat down, taking my first real breath in what seems like many days but is probably just a matter of twenty-four little hours. Was it just yesterday when I snuck into the basement and stole the red folder? Just yesterday when I stole Mom's car and twenty dollars, and Evvy and I rode off into the sunset?

The air is sweet and fresh, and the horizon is many hills away. The storm washed away a lot of the snow, leaving slushy puddles and the smell of cold mud. A lot of leaves and some small tree branches got knocked down by the storm last night, but many remain on the trees, and already there are hints of orange and red creeping in. These trees are full of birds, and their songs fill the air with joy. They stretch the wings to the sun, drying their feathers. They rode out the storm. We did, too, but I'm not quite that happy.

This isn't a dream. Maybe Evvy and I didn't drown in the waters off the ship, but we also didn't wake up in our own beds with Scarecrow and Tinman leaning in the window. We need to get out of here, but how? There's no cell service up here. The car is completely blocked by the downed oak tree. There is no gas station for miles around. Who knows which way Warren's Dairy is, or, gosh, was it even there at all? This place has everything we could ever need, and yet it has nothing. Nothing but sky and storms and snow-peaked mountains as far as the eye can see. On a different day, I would be awed by the beauty of nature. Today I feel trapped by its enormity.

Evvy tosses my English notebook on the ground and slips in beside me. "We need a new plan."

A more intimate moment I could not have imagined. Her, me, Arpeggio, by the apple tree, finding breath and relief together. I don't ever want to stand up.

"Do you have a Kleenex?" she asks.

I shuffle through the pockets of the pajamas and find a Kleenex. It looks pretty clean. I split it with her.

She opens the notebook, and the page flips onto Mr. Harrison's lecture in English class: *forgiveness*, it reads. "Mmm. Not ready for that one yet." She flips again. *Natural* and *supernatural*. "See?" She grins. "It's working already. We now get to choose what world we want to be in. The natural or the supernatural. I think I will choose ...

hmm. Let me see. Yes. Natural. Definitely the natural world." She stands up and pulls her clothes back together, and I follow. She is all business, tossing her sweater onto a dry spot on the bench in front of the cabin, making a little nest, and sitting. I do the same, pulling off my sweatshirt and making a spot beside her. But not too close. She smiles at me, but underneath, I think she's pissed that I got her into this. Arpeggio curls up at our feet.

She crosses her legs and takes a new page, writing:

NATURAL:

Evvy   Teddy   Adrian   Arpeggio

across the top. Under her name, she writes: *Go for help.* "Here's what I'm thinking. If I can sneak out, maybe get down to the road, maybe I can hitch a ride with someone and get to some cell service."

"That road?" I point. "You sure?"

"You see any other road around here?"

"No, but, Evvy. That road made me crazy yesterday."

"Today is not yesterday. Today I have a clear head and new faith. Teddy, come on! We have to do something."

"OK. I also have an idea," I say.

"You do?"

I turn back the page and point to *supernatural.* I look over each shoulder and whisper, "First things first, we need a car. Our car. This place is too far from anything, and no one travels this road."

"Yeah, but that means we need to get that tree out from behind the car," Evvy turns the page back to *natural.*

"I know."

"It's too heavy for us to lift."

"Right."

"So ..." She points to *supernatural*. "What? Adrian can get his spirit friends to move it?"

"No." Now I point to supernatural. "What if we could find a saw. Since this place has everything, I'll bet you anything it is has one of those big saws."

Evvy looks around. "Maybe, girlfriend. Somehow ..."

"Somewhere. Like in a small shed out back."

"There's a small shed in the back?" Evvy asks, and I point to the page: *supernatural*. "This place has everything."

"You ever used one of those things? In the real world, the natural world, they're really dangerous."

"Kids! Breakfast is ready. Come and set the table."

I freeze in my shoes.

"Please, Evvy, don't leave me here."

"OK. Tell you what. You go in," Evvy says. She points to my name on the page. "Keep him occupied. I'll look around. See if I can find this imaginary shed with the imaginary saw."

"Deal." We fist-bump, and I whistle for Arpeggio to come with me, but he trots alongside Evvy. They make their way around to the back. She crouches low, staying under the windows and out of sight.

Dad is up with coffee brewing and apples frying on the stove. Dishes are piled high in the sink. I open the last can of tuna and put it into a bowl for Arpeggio.

"Wait!" He lunges for the bowl, but I snatch it away.

"It's. For. Arpeggio," I say.

"You're giving that? To the dog? That's our food."

"Not anymore it's not. It's in his bowl. That makes it his." Suddenly my blood runs hot. I fill my lungs with air till I think my temples are going to explode. I am so mad at him—for kidnapping Adrian, for luring us up here, for the storms, the tree, for that ugly grin smeared across his face. I look him right in the eye and stare him down. I am not as tall as him, but I am growing all the time.

He lifts his hands and shows me his palms. Yeah right. A gesture of goodwill, of comradery, of surrender, of "Fine. OK then. It's for the dog."

I put the bowl on the floor and throw the spoon into the sink with a clatter that could wake the dead. "I am going to wake Adrian. Excuse me." He steps out of my way, and I crawl up into the loft. Adrian's sleeping bag is even more knotted up than it was before. I perch beside him and touch his shoulder. "Adrian," I whisper in his ear. "Wake up, honey."

He startles and tightens his grip on his sleeping bag.

"Adrian," I lean over and whisper in his ear. "It's me. Teddy. Listen, Evvy and I have a plan."

"Evvy is here?"

"Yes, little buddy. We're still in the cabin, and Evvy is still here. Shh."

His grip loosens. He rolls over, facing me. His eyes are gummy and hazy. If I look past how repulsive they are, I can see that they're a lovely shade of pale blue. His hair, a burgundy color, has grown long, and it flops over his forehead. He could have been a really handsome kid.

"We're not home yet? I dreamt that we were home."

"No, little buddy. We're still up here. But come on. Get your shoes and come outside. I'll tell you."

I grab my shoes and Evvy's. I take Adrian by his elbow and lead him to the ladder and down the rungs. We weave past the kitchen area, past the table with five chairs, now four, over the morass of scribbles and discarded papers that litter the floor, and out into the cool morning sunshine. "Sun's out," I whisper.

"I can feel it."

Adrian huddles under the same apple tree that Evvy and I enjoyed this morning. He stands for what seems like whole minutes, a river pouring out of him. *This kid is awesome in so many ways.*

"Adrian," I whisper in his ear. "Evvy has gone to find a saw. Somehow, we are going to move that tree today. Remember? When we came and the tree fell behind the car in that awful wind?"

"When Dad pushed it, you mean."

He's even deeper in these weeds than I thought.

"You didn't see any other trees come down, did you? And you didn't see any scratches on the car, did you? And you saw how Dad opened his arms and called to the gods, didn't you?"

"If you say so."

"I do say so. Teddy." And now he looks as tall as me. "Ever since he got here, these bizarre things have been happening. He hums. He calls. And pow! You show up. He opens his arms and howls—and pow! The tree falls down. Explain them away to your heart's content, but there is something about this place that has magic, and Dad is right smack in the middle of it all. I don't think any of us are strong enough to break through his spell."

Arpeggio dances around the corner of the house and dashes up to Adrian, banging into his knees and nearly knocking this poor kid over. He kisses Adrian's nose and face, and Adrian kisses him back. "Arpeggio! Good morning, puppy!"

Evvy stumbles along behind, carrying an enormous piece of equipment.

"Score!" She pulls a cord, and the motor fires up. The roar of the engine rips through the quiet. She stumbles, but she holds on. "You were so right, Teddy. I don't know how this thing works, but somehow, if there is a God, we will make it work."

The door flies open, and Dad looms in the doorway. "And just what do you two think you're doing?"

"We're …" I start to answer, but the words get stuck in my throat, drowned out by the noise of the saw. My knees are like water.

"What? You think you're going to saw your way out of here? Go run to Mommy for help? No! Where did you find that?" he screams at us. "Give it to me!" He lunges at her, grabbing at the enormous saw.

The buzz whirrs, and Evvy holds her own, her grip like a vice.

"I said …" Dad yells, twisting with her.

And the two of them, muscle for muscle, grip the saw. I try to get in and help Evvy, but the swing of the blade is too close, and it is all I can do to duck out of the way. Dad roars, a deep, rumbling roar, grips the cord, and with all his might, he pulls. The engine sputters and goes quiet. He throws it, and it lands with a clatter in the tall grass.

Evvy looks at the poor, bedraggled saw, a corpse of twisted metal lying in the grass. If a saw could weep …

"I said breakfast is ready. Now come on. All of you. Come in and eat." He stares at Evvy.

Evvy opens her mouth. I think she is going to say something, but then she closes it again. She slumps into her shoulders, walks over to her sweater lying in the grass, and puts it on.

"Ahoy, up there!"

Everything stops. Everyone looks. Someone, an apparition? A man, clean-shaven, hair combed, in a white button shirt, open at the collar, and a linen suit, is walking up the gravel path toward us. Suddenly he stops, shields his eyes from the sun.

"Teddy? Adrian? Meet your uncle Tony."

CHAPTER 22

UNCLE TONY

The man on the gravel path stares in disbelief. "I'm sorry. Do I know you?"

"Sure shootin', Anthony. It's me. Your brother." Dad doesn't run down the gravel path, arms open, ready to greet his brother, who he hasn't seen in years. He doesn't slap his knee in amazement. He doesn't even laugh. He stands there, by the apple tree, that creepy, omniscient grin in his cheeks, his tall shadow stretching out before him, his arms folded neatly across his chest.

"Sullivan? Well, I'll be." The man on the gravel path hurries now, his feet unsure of the path beneath him, but he is moving nonetheless. He stands in front of Dad, staring at him for a full minute, opening the bathrobe, pushing his hair aside, staring. "I mean, I'll be damned. You haven't changed a bit." He wraps his arms around my dad and gives him a big hug. Dad hugs back. I think. The man on the gravel path steps back, looks at him again, laughs again, and then it's another big hug. "Unbelievable. My boss told me that Harriet called the

restaurant, but never in a million years ... My God. Sullivan Carson."
He grins and hugs my dad again.

"Do you know this guy?" Evvy asks.

"Never seen him before," I say. "But if it's who I think it is, Mom
told me about him a few days ago."

"Well! God sure as heck works in mysterious ways, doesn't He?"
The man on the gravel path slaps his knee, claps his hands, spins
around, and laughs again. "Doesn't this just beat all? Do you know,
I've been driving up and down this road for the last two hours, my
GPS taking me this way and then that way and then this way again.
I was as scared as a rabbit in a tiger cage, but then I said to myself,
'Tony. Let go and let God. He'll lead you out of the wilderness.' And
then my car, well, all of a sudden, it ran out of gas. Right down there.
At the bottom of the hill. Can you believe it? I thought I was a goner
for sure. Some hillbilly's going to come out of the woods and shoot
me. Or some truck's going to come barreling through and squish me
flatter than the Nevada desert."

He looks back at the road, his long arm sweeping the landscape,
and we all turn and look for the kamikaze truck careening down the
road, ever on the lookout for someone to squish. He puts his hands together and bows his head. For a minute, I think he's praying, because
when he turns back to speak with us, he is a much more humble man.

"Because then, just then, I'm telling you, Sullivan, it was a miracle. I saw the smoke in the chimney, and I thought, *Yeah. OK. God
knows what He's doing with me, and He will provide. There are people
up there. They will kill me or they will help me.* 'And, Anthony,' I said
to myself, 'believe in our Lord Jesus Christ, for He is your savior.' And
look where I am. It's a miracle!" He takes another step back and looks

at my dad. "You look pretty good, Sullivan. Even with that crazy-ass haircut and beard. Gosh, what's it been. Ten years?"

"More," Dad says. "Anthony. This is my daughter, Edwina, and her little friend … I'm sorry. What's your name?"

Evvy stands up and puts her hand out. "Evvy," she says. "Evermore Martinez."

Uncle Tony lifts his eyebrows in a gesture of pure condensation. "That's a mighty unusual name." Evvy flashes a nasty dagger look at the two men. Uncle Tony bows slightly and takes her hand. "Anthony Carson. Very nice to meet you."

"Teddy?" Dad says. "Say hello to your uncle Tony."

I don't move. "Hi."

"Oh, my. You must be, what? Thirteen? Fourteen? It has been a long time, Sully."

"Sixteen," I say. "I'm sixteen years old."

"Harriet and I looked for you when she was born. Heard you were out of prison. But there was not a trace of you."

"Yeah, well, that's a long story."

"I'm sure it is," Dad says. "And that one. Over there." Dad points, his finger flapping off his wrist. "That's my son, Adrian."

"Well …" Uncle Tony waves. "I am certainly pleased to make your acquaintance."

"He can't see you. He's blind," Dad says.

Adrian curls in next to me, as tight as he can. "Hi," he squeaks, still flapping.

"Yup. You raised 'em right, Sullivan," Uncle Tony says and laughs. "Always up there with the best of manners for greeting a long, lost uncle." He looks around. "You don't happen to have a tank of gas around here, do you? I'm supposed to be at a business meeting at eleven o'clock. We're opening a new restaurant at the casino in Springfield. The meeting's somewhere near here. Well," he says, laughing, "I thought it was near here. Hard to tell up in these mountains. It's in some little Podunk, washed-up town—no, wait. I have it here." He pulls out a slip of paper. "That's it. Crystal Falls. Ha! How could I forget a name like that?"

My dad smiles. "Gas? No. But we have some breakfast ready if you'd like to join us."

"Breakfast? Well, my word, God really does provide, doesn't He? Yes." Uncle Tony wraps his long arm around Dad's shoulder, and the two men turn and head into the cabin, heads bowed. Uncle Tony stops at the doorway. "This your place, Sullivan? How long you been here?"

"Oh. Not very long. We have another place. In town."

"Well, this … it's nice. In a rustic sort of way." He slaps my dad on the back and laughs again as the two of them disappear into the cabin like old friends.

Adrian, Evvy, and I look at one another.

"That was the cold wind," Adrian says. "The guy that Dad's been waiting for."

CHAPTER 23

THE BROTHERS' REUNION

I look at my little brother. "He's guilt and shame?"

"Yup."

"And this was Dad's plan? To lure Uncle Tony up here?"

Adrian nods. "That's what he's been working on."

I laugh. "All these last months? All those twisted scribbles?"

"And all that humming."

"And I thought he was just depressed. What fools he makes of us all!" I turn to Evvy to explain. "For the last, I don't know how many weeks, maybe? Months? For a long time now, he would not come out of his room. We had to tiptoe around the house while he slept, like all the time."

"Yeah." Adrian rubs his little, diabolical hands together. "Except he wasn't sleeping, was he? He was planning. Plotting. Scheming. Scribbling. Day after day, thinking about Koluscap and magic and sorcery and the conjuring of weather. Oh, yeah. He's been working on this one for a while. His chance to exact revenge on his brother for years of harm and pain."

"I guess it worked," I say.

"You can't honestly believe what you're saying, do you?" Evvy asks. "You think your father has these"—she waves her hands and looks to the sky for impossible words—"supernatural, hocus-pocus powers? You heard that guy. He was looking for Crystal Falls, and he got lost. It's the same thing that happened with us. These mountain roads are incredibly confusing."

Adrian starts to hum and shift from one foot to another, flapping his hand across his nose. I wrap my arm around him.

"No. Of course not. We don't believe that, do we, Adrian?"

Hum. Shift. Hum.

"Good. End of story. Now, new plan." Evvy picks up the saw and turns it over. She is one with this piece of machinery. "You two go inside and distract them. Do something about breakfast or something. Keep it simple. I'm going to figure this contraption out. Try to get us out of here."

"I think he pulled the cord out."

"Really? When?"

"When he tried to wrestle it away. Do you want my help?" I ask. "Adrian can distract them as well as me."

"No."

That's it. A single word. It probably shouldn't hurt as much as it does. But it hangs in the air. Curt and tight. She doesn't look at me, doesn't smile. Just says no. Plain and simple. No.

"Oh," I say. "OK."

Adrian, Arpeggio, and I step into the dark cabin. At first, I can't see anything but outlines and shadows. A cold wind blows through.

Dad leans against the wall by the fireplace. His arms folded across his chest. Dust swirls in the beam of sunshine behind him. Like a halo. The apples that he made for breakfast are burned to a crisp. Uncle Tony is mixing a drink.

"You got it all right here, Sull," Uncle Tony says. "Yup. Every little thing that a man might need for a couple good martinis: gin, dry vermouth, sweet vermouth, and"—he reaches into the back of the pantry—"did you see these buried in the back here? Yup. Even a jar of olives." He holds it up to the window, and the sun pours through, making a sickly green rainbow on the floor. I don't know who this guy thinks he is, but he cradles the jar with both hands, the way a priest would hold a communion cup. "And did you see this? Right here. Under the cabinet. A rifle." He picks it up and smells the nose. "Yup. Smells like it's loaded too."

"What the hell? How on earth did it get there?" Dad grabs the rifle and stands it back up in the corner. "Did I move it?" He lifts his hands, trying to levitate it, and it topples onto the floor. He grins, puffs his chest out, and tries again, but Uncle Tony interrupts him.

"You have to believe, Sullivan. That has always been your problem, you know. Believe. With all your heart. Because when you do, God really does work in mysterious ways." He opens the jar with a pop and slips an olive into his glass. Never mind that it is probably about ten o'clock in the morning. He hands one glass to Dad and lifts the other one. "Cheers, Sullivan. It's good to see you again."

"Cheers, Anthony." They each take a sip. Dad glances at the rifle in the corner and then at his brother, glaring over the rim of his glass.

Uncle Tony smacks his lips. "Mmm. Perfecto! God brought me here, and now He has provided me with a perfect martini."

"You never married?" Dad asks.

"Nope. Never did. I like my freedom. If things get too hot, I can pack my bags and slide out of town." He slides his free hand through the air and laughs. "Nice and quiet. I guess you tied the knot though. And got two fine specimens in the process too. Well, I guess that means congratulations are in order." He sits in the overstuffed chair and puts his feet up on the cot, crossing them at the ankles. He doesn't take his shoes off. He lifts his glass and takes another sip.

"Yes. I did. I looked for you when we got married and again when Teddy was born. I thought you might come visit. You know. Witness my life. Meet my first child. I thought we could, you know, try to reconcile."

"Yeah. I served my time, did my year on parole, but then it's Nevada. Home of gambling and prostitution, the land where anything goes. You play your cards right, you can get away with most anything."

I clean the frying pan and cut up more apples, all the while watching Dad out of the corner of my eye. He says nothing, but I feel his hurt. Uncle Tony is his brother. He should have been there at the big times to share in the joy and sorrow.

"Oh, come on, Sullivan, You know how the system works. You keep your nose clean, you can kind of slide out of view. And that's just what I did." He laughs and takes another sip. "Yeah. I did my time. I washed dishes for a year like a good parolee, and when I graduated, I said sayonara and disappeared. Evaporated, you might say. Drifted around. Alaska, the Yukon. I had finally become my own free spirit, going whichever way the wind blew me. Psithurism. Your know that word, Sull?"

"Can't say as I do."

"The sound of the wind in the trees. That's what it means. It's a beautiful word, isn't it? 'Cause if you listen, I mean really listen, you can hear God singing."

"Adrian and I will make a fresh breakfast," I say. But the men don't hear me. Or they don't care. I don't think they know we're standing here.

"Can you finish cutting these?" I ask Adrian. "Without cutting yourself?"

He shifts from foot to foot, but he nods. "I think so."

"Good. I'm going outside to pick some more. And, Adrian? Listen to what they're saying."

He nods again.

"Teddy?"

"I won't be long. I promise."

I step outside. Evvy sits, cross-legged, under the apple tree. She has that huge saw in her lap. She's turning it over and over.

I sit beside her. "They have martinis. They're talking."

She doesn't look at me. "You're right. He pulled the cord out when he grabbed it from me." She throws it on the ground in front of her, and the clatter of dead metal echoes off the mountains. "Because for the life of me, I cannot figure out how to get it to start again."

I pick up the saw and turn it over in my lap, heaving with each turn. This thing must weight thirty pounds, a bottom-heavy weight. Even if we could get it started, how on earth would we saw that huge tree branch? As futile as all this is, at least I can look like I'm doing something. I flip switches and turn knobs and push things that can't be pushed.

"I'm getting out of here," Evvy announces. "I'll walk if I have to, or hitch a ride if I can. But I'm going to turn right at the foot of the gravel driveway and start walking. Something is bound to show up sooner or later."

"You're not afraid of the kamikaze trucks knocking you down?"

"Teddy!"

"It was a joke, Evvy. I'm sorry."

"Not in the mood." She turns away from me, gazing out past the car and the tree and onto the road. She still won't look at me.

"Evvy. Please stay. We'll think of something."

"Teddy. I can't breathe. I don't know any more what is real and what is not. I don't think you know either. But you saw him. He came right at me. He would have pushed me to the ground and … and I don't know what. So, for these last minutes, I've been sitting up here, looking at the car, at that old tree, trying to make some small sense of what happened. There was a wind, yes. But your dad, Teddy. Howling to the gods like that? And then—crack! And this tree that has stood for probably two hundred years through hurricanes and tornadoes and blizzards—suddenly this branch comes down? Right there? Right in front of the car? You think he has these … powers? The branch was dead, Teddy. It was ready to go, but …"

I hang my head. An old, familiar shame clings to every pore of my skin. I mumble, "I don't know."

"I don't either. But, Teddy, this morning I am honestly scared of him. He thinks he has these powers. He thinks he's infallible. And worst of all, he thinks he's right. And that makes him unpredictable. No. We need a new plan. Supernatural is not going to work. Natural is all we have left. I don't have a car, but I have my feet. I'm sorry." She stands up and brushes the leaves and grass off her sweatpants. "I'm leaving."

"At least let me come with you." I stand up and try to take her hand, but she pulls it back.

"No."

"No? But, Evvy—"

"Think about it, Teddy. If you come, then your dog comes. If your dog comes, then Adrian comes. If Adrian comes, then your father roars out of the house and, and, I don't know what he does, but I don't like it."

"OK," I say. "Good luck." I lean over to kiss her, but she is already walking down the gravel path.

She stops and turns. Maybe she'll give me that kiss after all. "You got your phone with you? Mine's in the loft. I don't want to go in there."

I hand her my phone, and she takes it, powering it on. "Fabulous. It's got a little bit of battery left, I think." No smile. No sweet kiss. Just a strong will to hike down the gravel path to the road.

I watch her until she disappears from sight and even a little longer. I keep thinking she'll come back, she'll walk back up the gravel path and say, "I have an idea! A new plan!" But she doesn't, and the silence of the whole valley hangs heavy on my shoulders once again.

I pick some more apples from the tree, our tree, and step back inside. They didn't even notice that I was missing. Uncle Tony is mixing a second martini.

"Now. Where was I?"

"You burned our house down."

"Oh yes. That. You know, Sull, those two years in prison after that little snafu—they were the best thing that could have happened to me. I found God. Or rather, God found me. Yup. And our Lord and Savior Jesus Christ. Right there in cell block number nine hundred forty-eight. And my life changed. Just like that." He snaps his fingers with one hand and lifts his glass for another sip with the other. "I quit gambling. Yup. I sure did. And believe you me, I couldn't have done it without the help of that man upstairs. Course, I started drinking, but that wasn't till I got out and was free of the evil system. Stand up straight, Sullivan. You're slouching."

"You gambled my life away. My life! My house! You lost it in a hot second and then burned it down. My papers! Gone! Because you lost to three queens."

"Yeah. I never did trust women. Well, I paid my dues. Eight years. That's what the judge gave me, and after two years, they let me out. 'Good behavior,' they said." He air quotes with his free hand and sashays back to the chair. He flops into it, and dust fills the shaft of sunlight. "Yup. Two years. That's what I did. Another year for probation, and I learned my lesson. I don't owe anyone anything, but if it makes you feel better, well, yeah, sorry about the house. There. You feel better?"

Neither man says anything.

I put my hand on Adrian's shoulder. "Nice job with the apples, little buddy." I lean over and whisper in his ear. "Evvy has gone for help,"

"How?" he whispers back.

"On foot."

"Teddy? I'm scared. What's Dad really up to?"

"I don't know."

"So, what's up with that breakfast I was promised, hey?" Uncle Tony picks up his glass in a gesture of a toast. "You want one?" he asks.

"No, thanks," I tell him. "The apples burned, so I'm cooking some fresh ones. It shouldn't be too long," I say. To Adrian, I whisper, "We have to keep them distracted. Give Evvy a chance to find her way."

"So, three years ago—was it three years ago?" He counts on his fingers. "Anyway, a while back, I wandered back to the old casino. Manager gave me my job back. Just like that." He snaps his fingers again. Things seem to happen so easily for Uncle Tony. "And now," he says, laughing. "You remember that job you had at the end?"

"Yeah. I was the manager of Fantasy Island. I remember it well."

"Yeah. Fantasy Island. Great place. Well now the restaurant has been rehabbed, and they still have those obnoxious birds yapping all the time, but would you believe it? The job is mine! Isn't that the funniest thing you ever heard?"

Dad doesn't laugh. He swoops his arm through the sunlight, and the dust settles over Uncle Tony. "Yup. Just the funniest."

Uncle Tony yawns. "Oh yeah. I think the morning of driving around and the excitement of seeing you again, well, let's say I should take a little nap."

"Good idea." Dad leaves his post at the fireplace. On his way out of the cabin, he taps out a rhythm with his fingers on the table, whistles a simple tune, grins at me and Adrian, grabs the rifle from off the floor, and, head high, says, "I'm going out."

"But, Dad. What about breakfast?"

And he slides into the great outdoors. Uncle Tony doesn't follow him. Doesn't turn around. Doesn't even move from the chair. I hold my breath, waiting to see what will happen, and in a few minutes, a soft, sloppy snore rises out of the crocheted blanket.

"He's asleep," I say, and Adrian nods.

The whole cabin seems to sleep. I fish around in the cupboard and find some dry raisins, cinnamon, and parsley. It all feels a little odd, but I toss the rice into the skillet with the apples, add water, the raisins, and spices, and cover it.

Outside the window, nothing stirs. The wind from last night has died down. No trucks rumble up the road. No planes fly overhead. A blue jay perches in the apple tree, staring at me and Adrian through the window. It gets Arpeggio's attention, but soon it grows bored and flies off.

"What if she gets lost?" Adrian asks.

"She can't get lost. She's Evvy."

CHAPTER 24

HUNTING

"Come on, Adrian. Let's you and me clean this place up."

"Clean?"

"Yes. We have to call on our own gods now and pray Evvy is going to find someone, that help is going to come. If we clean—"

"Fine. What do we have to do?"

"Can you wash dishes?"

"I've never done it."

"Well, I promise it won't turn you into a fag if you do some women's work." He wipes his eyes with his dirty sleeve. "Sorry. That was supposed to be funny. I'm not doing very well with my jokes this morning. Come on. I'll show you."

I lead him to the sink and put his hand on the pump. He grins and wriggles as the long arm of the pump moves up and then he pushes it down with a *sploosh*. We fill the sink and add some soap, and he stands there, pushing soap around last night's plates and forks.

I find a broom in the corner and pretend to sweep, but all it does is kick up dust. I pick the papers up off the floor: the spirals, the scribbles, the notes in the margin. I turn the papers over and over in my hands, and there are the words: "Fantasy Island." "Tony." "Las Vegas." Now it all makes sense.

"Adrian?" I whisper in his ear so as not too wake the man in the overstuffed chair. I still can't believe he's my uncle. "The spirit of Uncle Tony—was that the spirit you felt? The one that you said was drawing near?"

"That's what I've been trying to tell you. When he was mixing that—what was it?"

"A martini."

"So early in the morning?"

"I know," I say. "The smell of it made me want to gag."

"When he was doing it, did you feel the cold wind?"

I think back. "I think I did. I thought it was a draft."

"No. It came up through the floor. That cold wind. He laughs a lot, but underneath, I can smell his guilt and shame."

"Hard to believe that's what he's feeling. He's arrogant beyond belief," I say. "Are you double dog sure he's the 'really big thing' that Dad had planned for today?"

"I think so."

"It's starting to make sense, in a totally no-sense kind of way. One more question: last night, when you went outside with Dad, and you hummed with him, were you calling Tony's spirit here?"

"I don't know. I mean, I think that's what Dad thinks."

"And was it something you did the night before Evvy and I showed up?"

"Oh, Teddy. I'm so sorry. If I had known—"

"It's not your fault, Adrian."

"It's just that …" He starts shifting and flapping again. I grab his hand, and he stops.

"Talk to me, Adrian. What happened?"

"He's so taken with himself. He's convinced his stupid humming can raise a storm, bring down a tree, and conjure you and Evvy and Uncle Tony to the cabin. And the more this stuff happens, the more he believes the world revolves around him. Teddy? I don't know what to do. Do we pity him or fear him?"

"Or both? At the moment, I hate him. I hate that he did this to you and to us, and that no one can find us, and even though Detective Malloy called hospitals and motels and shelters, there was no sign of you. It's like you vanished off the face of the earth. And he doesn't care. He thinks it's fun. You must have been terrified."

"The way he sits at that table, up all night, humming like a cicada, whistling, the kerosene lamp hissing, and paper flying in every direction. I was afraid he was going to burn this place down."

He wraps his arm around my waist, and I put my arm around his shoulder, and we stand together, the way we have stood for so many years: Brother. Sister. A tiny fortress against the storm.

"But you know," Adrian continues, "I've never known him to be so alive or so happy. He has endless energy, and then he collapses in a heap for what—three hours? Maybe four? Time. That's all I know. Empty time. The coyotes howl and scratch at the door. The owls hoot. It's like I'm in a dream, and I want to wake up and be home and hear you knocking on my door, saying, 'Come on, Adrian. Time to get up. We have school.'"

I laugh. "I never thought I would miss that little ritual."

"Me neither. You're such a pain."

I laugh.

"You came close this morning, you know, waking me up and all and telling me about Evvy. For a hot minute, I thought I was home. But then, we're still here, aren't we?"

"Maybe Evvy will find help."

"Maybe. She's been gone a long time," Adrian says.

"I know."

"Do you think she's OK?"

I take Adrian in both arms now and hold him tight, his tender body trembling against mine. I don't know how to be the grown-up here. I don't know how to make decisions. I don't know how to be brave. But I say to him, "I hope so."

I turn the heat off of the apples and rice. I'm not sure this day is ever going to get started. And if it doesn't get started, it isn't going to end.

Pop!

My knees turn to water. "What was that?"

"That was Dad with his gun."

"Arpeggio!" I call into the emptiness of the cabin. "Arpeggio!" But he isn't here. He's not on the rug or on the papers or under the table or in the trunk of clothes. "Arpeggio!" I run outside, and he bounds up to me, up the gravel path and into my arms. He licks my face and wags his stumpy tail. "No, puppy. You must stay close. It's not safe here."

"Anyone here?" the man in the overstuffed chair calls into the empty cabin.

Oh, God. Now Uncle Tony's awake.

And indeed, he is. He stumbles outside, crawling in behind the apple tree and turning his back to us. I try to turn away, to not see him or hear him, but it's impossible. In the quiet of the mountains, he echoes in every direction.

He yawns and stretches. "Oh, my. I must have fallen asleep in there. All that driving around in circles, and then this clean mountain air. Don't know when I've felt so relaxed. Where's your little friend?" he asks.

"Evvy? She's, um, she's around," I lie. "Yeah. She'll be back soon."

"Mmm. I see. Yes." He looks around. "It's just you two? How about your dad?"

Adrian presses his small body next to mine. "Dad went out hunting," Adrian says. "Didn't you hear him shooting off that gun of his? He'll be back soon, and if anything should happen to us—"

"Woah. Hold on, kids. I ain't going to hurt you." He zips his pants and crawls back out, stretching his arms against the sky. "Is there any coffee?"

"Dad made some, but that was a while ago," I say.

"Oh. That's OK. Whatever it is, whatever it's like. Don't matter none to me, so long as it's coffee. And was there an offer for breakfast?"

"We're waiting for Dad."

All three of us, four if you count Arpeggio, and I always do, turn toward a narrow trail into the woods. Something or someone is rumbling down the path, crashing through tree branches. I grip Adrian's arm and breathe long, slow breaths, desperately trying to slow my heart for whatever is going to come out.

"Sullivan! Ha!" Uncle Tony laughs.

Yeah. It's Dad with nothing in his hands but a hunting rifle.

"Good to see you, old chum. I thought for sure you were a bear coming to eat us. Did you catch anything with all that huff and puff shootin'?"

"Very funny. Rabbit's dry meat anyhow." He steps past us and walks into the cabin, mumbling something I can't understand. Uncle Tony follows him.

"So, Sullivan. How about that breakfast, huh?"

There is a clattering of tin plates and forks. Whatever happens now, I don't care. Let the men shoot each other. Let them kiss and make up. Let the whole cabin burn to the ground. I give up. None of it matters anymore.

CHAPTER 25

YELLOW

I pick up my sweatshirt and wrap it around Adrian's shoulders. We sit together on the bench, a cold October breeze blowing through the warmth of the sun. Arpeggio curls up at our feet. Dad and Uncle Tony are back at it again, arguing about something, but for this one moment, their voices don't mean anything. They can be very far away. Me. Adrian. Arpeggio. In a day that is almost as quiet as it is immense. The sky is azure blue from one side of the horizon to the next. Yellow leaves shudder in the breeze. The sun is warm on our faces. A ladybug crawls up a blade of grass. Arpeggio stares at it, observing every flicker of the antenna.

"Psithurism," I tell him. "This is an Uncle Tony word. It means the sound of wind in the trees."

Adrian takes a deep breath. "Psithurism," he says, letting the word sit on his tongue like fresh ice cream. "It smells like fall. Is it fall?"

"Yes, little buddy. It's October. Fall in the mountains. Can you hear the breeze?"

"Yeah. But I miss colors," he says. "I remember, they used to be so pretty. And so many of them. I remember that too."

"Do you see them in your dreams?"

"Sometimes. But when I wake up, they all seem to run away. I remember the people, sometimes, and the things that happen, but the colors?" His hands dance in front of his face. "They're like fairies. They disappear under the mushrooms." And his hands slither into the horizon.

I laugh. "I've always taken them for granted."

"Tell me, Teddy. What colors do you see?"

"Oh. There are so many. It's fall, and the trees are turning all these beautiful colors. The mountains look like a fire—all red and orange and yellow."

"Red?"

"Yeah. Some of them are red and loud, like a fire engine peeling through the streets." I make a soft sound like a siren wheeling up the street.

Adrian laughs. "That's funny."

"And some of them are red and quiet, like when you snuggle in real close and you can hear my heart beating."

Adrian snuggles in close, listening to my heart. Dad and Uncle Tony talk, and for a second, I strain to hear what they are saying, but their voices are muffled. I wrap in close. "Or like when the embers in the fire die down, and it fills the room with warmth. Can you feel the glow of the fire?"

"I can."

"And then there is yellow," I say. "The birch trees turn yellow. The birch trees are the ones with the soft paper bark."

Adrian nods. His body relaxes in my arms.

"And yellow is, gee, let me see—yellow is the taste of fresh corn in August. With butter melting all over it. It's sticky. And yellow is sweet, like ripe bananas. Well, before they get too mushy."

"Yellow is the sun. I remember that," Adrian says.

"Yes. And today it's soft and warm."

"I think I'd like to sleep in yellow," Adrian says.

"Yeah. I'd be happy to sleep in my own bed," I say.

We sit side by side for the longest time, while the cicadas whir in the trees. Blue jays come and go. Robins and cardinals fill the air with song. Every color, large and small, is alive.

"Teddy?" Adrian takes my hand. "Thanks for coming. I'm not afraid of him when you're around."

I give his hand a squeeze. "You're something else, Adrian. Like no one I've ever met."

A chipmunk rustles in the tall grass and runs up a tree.

"Who's coming?" Adrian asks.

"No one. That was a chipmunk."

"No. Really. Someone's coming."

And damn if he isn't right. It's Evvy walking back up the gravel path.

"You came back."

"I never left." Evvy squeezes in next to Adrian. She crosses her legs and puts her head in her hands, shaking it. "I've been walking in circles. I think I'm going in one direction, and then I'm going in another. I would try to keep going, but then I was back over the same ground I covered. I'm telling you, Teddy. There's something about this place that is not right.

"But for a second there, I must have been a half mile or so, that way, I think." She points to the right. "I thought I got some cell service. Your phone pinged, like it was turning on. I tried to text my mom, but then it was gone. Supernatural didn't work. Your dad pulled the starter cord right out of the saw. And that means that natural didn't work. I'm still going in circles. God, Teddy. How are we ever going to get out of here?"

"Kids. Come on. Breakfast is ready."

CHAPTER 26

FIVE CHAIRS

Suddenly, sunlight is everywhere in the cabin. It pours in through the door, the dirty windows, the cracks in the walls. It's a warm, yellow, welcoming light. The papers from the floor have been assembled into a neat pile at the foot of the cot, and the floor is clean. The kitchen is tidy. The lid of the trunk is closed. The rifle is perched in the corner. Embers glow in the fireplace.

Uncle Tony stands at the foot of the table. He grips the back of the chair. Dad stands at the head. He's still wearing that red bathrobe over his clothes, but his hair is combed and his beard is less of a mess. He looks like a high priest. Or like that's what he's trying to look like. He looks a little ridiculous, if you ask me.

"Dad?" I ask. "What's going on?"

Dad smiles. "It's time for us all to sit now, to sit together in these five chairs." His hands are folded at his waist, and with a great sweep, he opens his arms and motions for us to sit in these spots designated for each one of us. Uncle Tony sits, and I sit, and dutifully we take our positions, folding our own hands on the table, waiting for the prayer to begin. And after a moment, Evvy sits. Yes. This is why there are five chairs. This meal—some meal—we are his pentagram. It was all part of his grand master plan. One of those scribbles with words.

Adrian does not sit. He leans over and whispers to Evvy, "He's going to turn us all into turtles and throw us into the fire."

"At this point," she whispers back, "anything is possible." She helps Adrian with his chair, but he shifts around the cabin, finally coming to a stop by the overstuffed chair.

"Adrian?" Dad says. His voice is stern. "I'm asking you to sit. Enjoy some of this wonderful breakfast that your sister made."

"I'm not hungry," he says.

"Adrian?"

"There's nothing more you can do to me, Dad. You can beat me if you want. Kill me if you need to, but I'm not going to sit at your table."

Everyone gets quiet and solemn. Arpeggio looks for more tuna in his bowl, and his tags clang against the metal while he licks the sides clean. We all pretend that a quiet stillness fills the cabin.

"Well, this looks and smells delicious." Uncle Tony takes our plates and serves us. My mouth waters, and suddenly I am really hungry. The rice and apples are still warm, and the smell of cinnamon floats over the table. I pick up my fork, but Uncle Tony glares at me, so I put it down again.

"Please, everyone. Eat. Teddy has made us a delicious breakfast."

We dive in like we haven't eaten in a week of Sundays, like a pack of racoons devouring fresh trash, our lips smacking. "This is delicious," Evvy mumbles, and Uncle Tony curls his nose and takes a sip of his—third? Fourth? Martini.

"Yes, very nice," he says.

I eat till there is nothing left on my plate, and then I look in the pan. I'm so hungry, it's all I can do to not eat it all.

I put down my fork and fold my hands in my lap. We look at Dad. Dad looks at us. Arpeggio scratches at the screen door.

"Shh, puppy." I put my finger over my lips. "Go lie down."

He lies down, his nose in the door.

"I was going to turn you all into mighty sea turtles," Dad says. "That was my original plan."

No one moves.

"Oh, relax. That was a joke." Dad laughs, but no one else does. "Now. Please. The reason why we are here today. Your uncle Tony. He is finally ready to apologize. Aren't you, Tony?"

Uncle Tony stares at my dad.

"No one cares, Dad," Adrian says. "No one cares what your stupid reasons are for all this hocus-pocus. No one cares anymore if it's power or forgiveness or world peace that you want. What you have done over these last days is unforgiveable, and you deserve to be left very, very alone. Alone! You're going to shrivel up into a dry—"

"Adrian!" I say.

"Shut up, Teddy. " Adrian pounds his heart. "Dad, it's coming for you. I can see it. In my heart. You're going to shrivel into a dry piece of ... of something. And then you are going to blow away, and you know what? No one is going to care. Do you hear me?"

"I hear you," Dad says.

Arpeggio scratches at the door.

"I think he wants to go out," Evvy says.

"I think he has to wait," I say. "Arpeggio! Lie down!" And he does.

"We're getting out of this place," Adrian hisses. He's fierce. "And you're going to be here, all by yourself. Alone. Forever."

"Alone?" Dad laughs. "You think that's anything new? Adrian Carson, you have no idea what it means to be alone, to feel like you're the only soul left alive in the world."

"I do know!" Adrian yells.

"I do too!" Dad slams his hand on the table, and everything jumps. "Sometimes, Adrian, sometimes the solitude is terrifying, an infinite night sky with no gravity. No place to hold on. But let me tell you. Sometimes it's my best friend, comforting even, to have nobody watching my every move, looking over my shoulder, asking questions, prying into my business. People want to open me up like a can of tuna. Peek inside me, pry their grubby little noses into me. They offer me one medication after another, and each one is great for a little while, but then I feel it in there, sucking out my soul. You might hate me and my mood swings and my depression, but I like me. My highs and lows mean I can reach from one end of the universe to the other. I can see everything."

His voice bounces off the walls of the cabin, and he stares at Adrian. I swear Adrian can see him. He stares right back, but his lip is twitching, and his little shoulders seem to melt into his hips.

"You all think you know so much about me, but you"—he sweeps his arm again—"none you have any idea. All my life, I have been haunted by people like you, always looking, always wondering, 'Are you all right, Sullivan? Do you need anything, Sullivan?' And underneath it, what they're not asking me is 'Are you going to flip out on me?' I can tell them I'm fine, but still they look. Still they wonder. Still they wait. Well, I'm sick of it! It stops here."

And then it is a loud pop! And for a moment, I am deaf. Everything is muffled, underwater, and I'm swimming. Nothing makes any sense. Evvy is at the door, holding Arpeggio. Uncle Tony is behind Dad, his arms around his chest, holding him tight. Adrian stands at the fire-place, the rifle in his hands. Smoke seeps from the barrel of the gun.

"No one cares!"

Arpeggio wriggles out of Evvy's arms and throws himself at the door, yelping and barking. He squeezes his nose into the door jamb, flips the door open and runs out, his muffled bark filling the skies.

"Arpeggio!" I leap to my feet and run after him, but he's gone. Vanished. "Arpeggio! Come!"

"Adrian?" Evvy says. Even though her voice is muffled, with her inside and me out here, I hear the shaking. "Can you give me the gun?"

"No!"

"Arpeggio!"

There is more barking—down by the road, I think—and a squealing of brakes and an ear-splitting howl.

And then silence.

"Arpeggio!" I run down the gravel path. Evvy is right behind me. She grabs my arm, and I reel.

"Teddy! Wait! You don't want to see it."

I rip out of her grasp and run down the path, calling his name, but he isn't there. I turn and run for the woods, screeching, but he isn't there either. I run to the back of the house and look around the shed where he and Evvy found the saw, but he isn't there.

Exhausted, out of ideas, I come back to the yard by the apple tree, and there on the gravel path is Arpeggio, trotting toward me, his stumpy tail high and wagging. He's panting. "Arpeggio!" I fall to my knees, and he runs in, wriggling and licking me up the side of my face.

And right behind him is Detective Malloy.

CHAPTER 27

COULD THIS BE REAL?

"Sullivan Carson! This is the police!"

I stare at the detective for the longest time. We all do. I can't believe he is right here in front of us. Walking up the gravel path. Getting closer with every step. But there he is, waving and grinning, and he seems to be real.

Detective Malloy's breath is heavy but steady. A younger man in a uniform bounces up the path behind him. The detective calls again, "Sullivan Carson. Are you in there? This is the police."

Silence rings the cabin.

The detective stops when he reaches us. He slides his sunglasses down his nose and looks at us with his steely gray eyes. He puts one hand on my shoulder, the other on Evvy's. "You must be Evvy Martinez." Evvy nods, tears swelling in her eyes. His hand is strong. It is warm. It has weight. It is solid and real. "I'm Detective Malloy from the Crystal Falls Police Department. You girls sure are a sight for sore eyes. You both OK?" he asks, and we nod, but honestly—OK? Do I even know what that means?

"Good." He looks at the door and then back at me. "We got a call this morning. Five o'clock maybe? From some kid who works at Warren's Dairy. He said he'd seen two girls looking for a father and son. They described your mother's car. That was you, wasn't it?"

I nod.

"Yeah. Well, me and the sergeant here"—he motions to the man behind him—"we've been driving around these hills since dawn, going from one hunter's lodge to the next. But then, like a miracle, we got a ping from a cell phone about an hour ago." He opens his phone and points at me. "Your cell phone, I think. We were on our way here when Arpeggio—that's his name, isn't it?" We nod. "He ran out right in front of us. I had to slam on my brakes so as to not hit him. He was barking and dancing. He ran up the little gravel road, then he ran down again. And, sure enough, he brought us up here." He leans down and scratches Arpeggio behind both his ears. "This is some dog you got here. I would swear on my mother's eyes that he knew exactly what he was doing."

I get down on my knees and wrap my arms around my dog. "Thank you," I whisper in his ear. "You're a good dog."

"Is your brother here too?" the detective asks, and I nod. He kneels down next to me and lifts my chin off my chest. "Oh, my. Is he OK?"

I nod.

"And your dad?" he asks, and I nod again. He steps back, his hand back on my shoulder. "Your mamma filled me in a little more on what's been happening lately. With your dad, I mean. And his meds. It sounds serious. Is it serious?"

I shrug my shoulders and squeeze Arpeggio. It's all so embarrassing. He's not supposed to know any of this. It's my family. It's private. "I guess."

"Yes," Evvy says. "It's serious. And have you talked to my mom?"

The detective nods. "Oh, yes. She called the station five times last night to see if there had been any word." He stands, brushing the grass and pollen from his knees. He offers me his hand. I take it, and he lifts me up. "Both your mammas are worried sick."

"I know." I reach my hand out to Evvy, giving her a tender squeeze.

She doesn't squeeze back. Instead, she asks the detective, "Can you get us out of here?"

"I can. Don't you worry." He's just about to ask me another question, but there is a crashing sound inside, a chair flung against a wall, the shattering of glass. The gun fires again, and Adrian runs outside, slamming the door behind him, the rifle in his hands.

"Teddy! Where are you?" he shrieks.

"Adrian!" I rush to the door with the detective close behind. I take him by the shoulder and lead him away from the door toward the little bench. "What happened?"

"I didn't hit him. I swear I didn't. I—" He grips the rifle, his skinny hands so strong now. "But something happened."

"It's OK, little buddy. Sit. You're safe here. Detective Malloy is here. He's come to take us home. Shh. Now"—I take hold of the rifle—"I've got this. You can let it go, Adrian."

And he does, mumbling something about Dad and vodka and maybe Uncle Tony again. I hand the rifle to the sergeant. "Do something with this." I practically screech this, but the sergeant starts down the hill, rifle in hand. He looks back once and then breaks into a run.

"And, Sergeant! Call for backup!" The detective bangs on the door. "Sullivan Carson! This is—"

The door flies open, and Dad steps outside, his very being filling the entire doorway. "Well, well, well. It's our boys in blue. How good of you to come. Would you like some coffee? We have a little left."

"Detective Malloy. Crystal Falls Police."

"I know who you are."

"Is there someone in there with you?" He tries to get in the door, but Dad steps in his way.

"Nope. Just us chickens." He runs his fingers through his hair, his ugly grin turning to something sticky sweet, so large it fills his face, and his eyes wrinkle. He is smooth and charming again, the very picture of innocence. "It's a beautiful morning, isn't it? The sky so clear, and the air so fresh. Makes you glad to be alive."

"Sullivan Carson. I'm sorry, but I have to place you under arrest."

"Really? Arrest?" He laughs. "On what charge?"

The detective smiles and cocks his head. "You serious?"

Dad mirrors the smile and the cocked head. "Why yes. I am."

"OK." The detective takes a step forward. "Let's start with kidnapping a minor, shall we? We'll see if that sticks. Then, if we're desperate, we can move to trespassing and unlawful breaking and entering. Possessing a firearm without a license. And I'm sure there are more charges where those came from."

"How about breakfast? We have some apples and rice. Teddy made it. It's delicious."

If I was confused before, it's nothing compared to what I am now. Is the same man who has kept us all prisoner? The one who called Adrian "Tortoise" and forced him to go out in the rain and hum circles around the mountains? This dad, the one standing by the door now, he's as nice a man as you would ever want to meet. Kind and welcoming and charming. Even I'm tempted to go inside and join him for coffee and apples.

Detective Malloy sidles up to him, his hand extended. "Mr. Carson? I'm not going to hurt you."

Dad puts his hands up, palms out, and the detective stops. "Adrian is my son. My legal, lawful son, so you can't charge me with kidnapping. And as for the ones about trespassing and breaking and entering? Pfft. Keep 'em. I worked with Emily Ackuin. Maybe you know her. She's Mohican. Lives up in North Adams. She told me all about this place. Said I could use it anytime. And what was the third one? Oh, right, the rifle. Sorry. Not mine. Was here when we got here. Sorry to waste your time, but we're kind of in the middle of something important here, so if you'll excuse us ..." He turns to go into the house, but the detective grabs him by the elbow.

Dad reels around, swinging his arm over the detective's head. A wind shivers by. "Don't. Come. Any. Closer. I'm warning you."

But the detective does go closer. Slow and easy, with a calm voice and a steady hand. The sergeant is right behind him, his hand hovering above the pistol in his belt. "It's over," the detective says. "Come on. We can get you some help."

"I'm sorry. You've come a long way for nothing, but I ain't coming, I tell you. I ain't going anywhere. This is my home now. I belong here. The rabbits, the crows, the wind—they need me. They need my magic and my ... my—and besides, Adrian wanted to come. Didn't you, boy?"

The detective turns and looks at Adrian, who doesn't say anything. He tucks in closer to me, hiding his face in my armpit.

"Cat's got his tongue, I'm afraid. I can tell you what happened though. That morning last week. If you're interested."

The detective doesn't look at Dad. He looks at Adrian and says, "Go on."

"Well. It was a Monday morning. I was up early. Baking cookies. Offered to drive Adrian to school, and there we were, just like old times, driving along and laughing, and suddenly I had this amazing idea. 'Adrian. How about you and I drive up to the mountains? Play hooky? We can get some ice cream,' I said, and he said, 'Sure,' and off we went. It was a gorgeous day, just like this one, and then I told him about this cabin that I knew and asked him if he'd want to check it out, and he said, 'Sure,' and one thing led to another." He laughs. "Funny, isn't it? How time gets away."

The detective kneels and takes Adrian's hand in his own. "Adrian? My name is Detective Malloy. I'm with the Crystal Falls Police. Your mom called me. She's pretty worried about you. Can I ask you a couple of questions?"

Adrian nods.

"Is that what happened?"

Dad clears his throat. "Go ahead, Tortoise. Tell him." The detective misses this little gesture, but Adrian doesn't. Dad stands tall, his arms stretched wide, palms out, ready to raise another storm.

"I … y … yes, sir."

"You sure? Is there anything you want to tell me?"

"No," Adrian squeaks. "Th … that's what ha … happened."

The detective stands up, squeezing Adrian's hand. "Well. OK then. I think we're all good here. You kids want a ride? We're heading back into town."

He doesn't have to ask us twice. I grab my backpack and notebook off the ground by the apple tree and start down the gravel path. Never mind my clothes or cleaning up. I'm gone. Evvy takes Adrian's hand, and Arpeggio dashes out in front, and just like that, we are halfway down the path.

But then, just then—damn! we were so close—the cabin door swings open, and there is Uncle Tony standing in the doorway, his linen suit still pressed and clean. He rubs his head. "Sullivan? Everything OK out here?"

The detective pulls his gun from the holster and looks at this apparition standing before him. "Hands up. Don't move."

Uncle Tony puts his hands up while the detective reaches into his back pocket and flips open his ID. "Detective Malloy of the Crystal Falls Police Department. Sergeant Johnson is back at the car." He stares at Uncle Tony. "May I ask, who are you?" like, *Are you an accomplice in all this?*

"Crystal Falls! Wow. This is a small world out here."

"Your name?"

"Sorry. Anthony Carson here." He steps forward, his hand extended to shake, but the detective does not take it. Does not stop piercing him with those eyes. "I'm Sullivan's brother. What happened?"

The detective lifts his pistol to his shoulder and steps into the doorway behind Uncle Tony. He squeezes the screen door open an inch and leans into the doorframe, peering inside to see if anyone else is there. "Maybe you can tell us," the detective says, his voice nice and steady. "Now, one more time. Is there anyone else inside?"

"There's no one else," Uncle Tony tells him. "Gosh. Oh, Lord, help me now. The last thing I remember is"—he rubs his temples, looking back inside the cabin—"yeah. Last thing I remember is a chair flying across the room. Must have clinked me, right here." He rubs his temples again. "Though I could have sworn I was under some kind of spell."

"You been here long?" the detective asks.

"Just since this morning. I'm … uh … you know," he says, laughing, "it's a pretty funny story, actually." He extends his hand again, but the detective does not laugh, and he does not take the hand. "You don't by any chance have an extra gallon or two of gas in your car, do you?"

"Sir?" The sergeant walks back up the hill. "Backup is on the way, sir."

The detective reaches for Dad again, but I can tell he's losing patience. His hand is shaking, and he's speaking through gritted teeth. "It's time, Sullivan."

"Don't touch me!" Dad flails, his arms flying in every direction. He takes a wide swing at the detective, but then he stops. His eyes scan the grass, stopping at Evvy. He begins to shift forward. His eyes are ablaze; his teeth are on edge. "You called them?"

"Dad. No." I try to step toward him, up the gravel path, but Adrian grips my sweatshirt.

"It wasn't like that, Detective," Adrian says. "Are you still here?"

"I'm right here, son. Go ahead."

"My dad … he made me come. He said if I didn't come, he'd kill Teddy's dog."

"Aarrgghh! Traitors! All of you!" Dad lifts his arms and howls, conjuring the wind, but nothing happens. He does it again. Still nothing. He does it a third time, his howl looping and twisting with anguish. A squirrel runs up the apple tree, chirring.

"Sullivan!" Uncle Tony cries. "Please. Stop."

Dad stiffens and smiles. "It's OK, Detective. I'm not going to hurt anyone." But he takes a step toward Adrian. "Am I, Adrian? Huh? Huh? Speak up, Tortoise." Step.

And that's when the detective steps in between Adrian and Dad, and Dad lunges at the detective, and then the two of them are on the ground, grunting and twisting around each other. It doesn't take a minute though before the detective grabs one arm and then the other, and out comes the cuffs.

Dad crumples into a heap on the ground, trembling. The detective stands, brushing his clothes. He's gasping for air. And … is he crying?

"You have the right to remain—"

There they are—two of the strongest, most powerful men I know, reduced to tears and terror in what? Three minutes? Twelve minutes? How quickly things turn. How quickly our lives that we have spent years building can crumble at our feet. A pile of rubble.

"Teddy?" my dad mumbles.

"Yes, Dad?" I approach him but not too close.

He nods and says something that sort of sounds like "Thank you," but it probably isn't that, and something else that sounds like "I haven't slept."

"I know, Dad."

He shakes his head. "Can you help me blow my nose?"

My head is spinning. More than anything, I don't want to get near him. He is flying one minute, crashing the next. What will he do next? Fly again? Lunge at me with his teeth?

"Is he OK?" Evvy asks.

"Do you have a Kleenex?"

She fishes around in her pocket and hands me one. It's been used a few times, but I flatten it out, good as new.

I try to wrap my arms around her, but she pulls away. "He says he hasn't slept."

"Really?" She looks at me, surprised that I am buying that line, and then she laughs. A snap of a "Ha!" And she claps her hands. "That's it? He hasn't slept?"

"Yup. That's it."

I hold the tissue up to Dad's nose. My heart pounding, my knees shaking. But all he does is blow. I wipe his nose.

"This is a mess." Evvy steps in behind me. "What's that poem?"

"What poem? What are you talking about?"

"The one about the falcon. That line about anarchy."

"Ah. Yeats. Yes. 'Mere anarchy is loosed upon the world.' Is that what this is?"

"Yeah," she says. "That sounds about right."

I put my hand on the small of her back, and this time she tenses, but she doesn't pull away.

CHAPTER 28

BLUE LIGHT

The silence is deeper than anything I have ever heard. It's not a quiet silence though. It's a silence that sits in the pit of your stomach and swells. A few leaves flutter in the breeze, a few birds start up with song, maybe something rustles in the underbrush. It's the silence of defeat.

The detective begins to explore the grounds. I don't know what he's looking for, but he's moving through the grass and down the gravel path.

"What happened?" Uncle Tony steps up to Evvy, Adrian, and me. We're all still huddled in together, real tight. Adrian clings to my shirt. Uncle Tony turns a full 360 degrees, surveying the landscape of broken souls. No one answers him because there is no answer. There's no sense to any of this, and so each one of us finds a way to look away.

"Wow. I always knew you were nuts, bro, but this …" He turns to us and straightens his shoulders. I think he's trying to muster up a little empathy here, but honestly, it doesn't matter. None of it matters.

None of it is real. I'm going to wake up, in my own bed, and say, "Ugh. What a horrible dream." Just like Dorothy did when she got back to Kansas. But it will be over. Mom will be headed off to work. Dad will be asleep. Me and Adrian and Arpeggio will walk to the river and skip some stones before winter comes.

"I tried to talk to him," Uncle Tony says. "You know. In there. Just now. I told him if he could open his heart to God and the teachings of the good Lord Jesus, he could give up all the meds and the doctors and the pain. He'd be free. I think that's when he threw the chair at me. I tried to duck, but I think he got me right here." He rubs his temple. "From what I could see in there, he broke the vodka bottle too. And maybe a few other things. The place is a bit of a mess, I'm afraid. Sorry."

"Yeah," I say, "this whole day has been a little wild."

"Sergeant?" Evvy asks. "What's going to happen to him?"

"Paramedics are on their way. They'll take him to the hospital, until we can get someone from mental health to evaluate him. Folks in the station, they know what's happening. Well, at least that Adrian was kidnapped and that you and Evvy were missing."

"Kidnapped? Really?" Uncle Tony takes a breath. Many breaths. "Oh, Lord God Savior. He didn't tell me that."

"Are we going to get out of here?" Evvy asks.

The sergeant nods. "Soon as the ambulance comes and we can sort all this out."

Silence settles back over the house again. It's like the cabin itself is breathing.

"Pretty close call with your car." Detective Malloy climbs back up the path. "I mean that oak tree. That just happened?"

Evvy and I look at each other. "Yeah. Last night. It's kind of hard to explain," I say.

"Dad did it," Adrian announces. "With his magic. He brought up the wind and knocked that branch right down."

That stops the detective. He takes out his notebook and his stub of a pencil and scratches his head. "I see. Yeah. OK. Still, that was a pretty ferocious wind last night, and by the looks of it, I'd says that branch has been dead for a while. But the car looks OK. I'll get the boys up here to get her free."

"Teddy is my hero," Adrian says. "Dad led her here with his magic spells, and she found us, and I was so scared, but as soon as she came, I started to feel so much better."

Flashing lights pierce the infinite stillness of the hills. And two men in white coats and two more men in uniform traipse up the hill. The men in white coats carry a stretcher. Straps dangle off the sides; buckles clip against the frame. One of them waves to the detective.

"Hey, Malloy. Hear you got a live one."

The detective nods and tilts his head in our direction, a signal for the guy in the white coat not to make any jokes. "This is his daughter, Edwina, his son, Adrian, and their friend Evermore."

"And Arpeggio," I add.

"Yes. And Arpeggio." The detective steps up to one of the men in white, his hand extended. The two men shake. "You got here really quickly," the detective says.

"Hospital's just the other side of Warren's Dairy. Pretty easy, you know? You kids OK?" But he doesn't wait for an answer. "This the guy?" the white coat asks. The detective nods. "Agitated?"

"He was. He's pretty subdued now."

"OK. We'll give him this anyhow. Make the ride a little easier."

The guy in the white coat nods to the guy in scrubs, and the guy in scrubs takes out a needle. He shoves it into Dad's arm, just below the shoulder. Dad unspools. He pees himself. He folds in half. The two men pick him up. Dad is floppy, like a wet fish. The detective takes the handcuffs off, and two men ease Dad onto the stretcher, strapping him in, "So he doesn't fall off," the white coat says.

And then, just like that, they're gone.

CHAPTER 29

HOME

It's all hugs and kisses and squeals of delight when we get home. Mom wraps her arms around me and then Adrian and then me again and says, "Are you OK?" and "You're so skinny! Have you eaten anything?" And I have tears streaming down my face, and I nod and say yes, and she asks Adrian, and he nods yes, and then she hugs us again, and she's crying, and then she makes some tea.

Adrian and Arpeggio and I wander the house like three lost ghosts. Sun pours through the dining room windows, exhausted from its journey of ninety-three million miles, ready to rest on the carpet. There's the dining room table. And my chair. And Adrian's. And … and Dad's chair. Up there at the head. Mom is chattering on about something.

"Well, you have to understand, I was really groggy because I had taken this sleeping pill for my migraine, you know, and it was dark by then, and that terrible wind, and I thought you must have gone to bed because the house was so quiet. But then, oh gosh, it must have been around nine o'clock, Evvy's mom called. She was very upset, as you can well imagine, and she came over, and of course the place was a mess, but she said it was all right, and did I need help with the dishes? Oh, goodness. She said It would do her good to have something to do, and so I said OK, but I was really so confused, but together we washed the dishes and waited, and then we looked for you everywhere. We even went into the woods calling for you. Then we called the detective. Are you listening, Teddy?"

"Yes, Mom." I wander into the kitchen and pick up Arpeggio's bowls. I fill one with fresh water and the other with food. I sit next to him while he eats. He eats so slowly. One kibble at a time. He picks it up. Chews it. Swallows. And then moves onto the next one.

"Needless to say, I wouldn't have slept at all, except that sleeping pill I took kicked in again, and then the detective came by about ten. He asked me a lot more questions, and then he was gone. Are you really listening to me, Teddy?"

"Yeah, Mom. Sorry. I'm a little tired, I think."

I text Evvy to say I am home safe and it's nice, and for the rest of the day and into the night, I sleep. Arpeggio curls at my feet, and when I flop, he shifts his weight.

Outside, the air is still, but in my dreams, the wind whistles in the trees. Branches crack and fly into the air. One branch grows wings and begins to soar in some odd widening gyre. Dad stands in a field, calling to the branch, but it does not come, and he fires the rifle. *Pop.*

I wake with a start, covered in sweat. I grope for my phone. It's 2:48. There is no message from Evvy.

Arpeggio squeaks, his feet running in place. He shakes and lifts his head, his eyes wide, looking at me.

"It's OK, puppy. We're home." I rub his back, and he rests his head and begins his soft, sloppy snores.

I lean back, but when I close my eyes, Dad is there, in his red robe, lighting a fire and pouring vodka on the floor.

"Morning." I stumble down the stairs. "What day is it? I'm completely lost in time."

"Sunday." Mom is at the sink washing dishes.

I slide past her and open the back door for Arpeggio. He scampers out, spinning circles around the backyard. "It's wonderful being home." The dog fills me with joy for being home, being safe, feeling rested. "Look how happy he is." I turn around and open my arms to give her a hug.

"Your father wants to see us," she tells me. "You, especially. He wants to see you."

I laugh. "I'll bet he does."

"This isn't a joke, Teddy." She crosses her arms over her chest. Real slow. Deliberate.

"I know that."

"You stole my car," she says. Hugs and kisses time is clearly over.

"I borrowed your car."

"I told you no. You did it anyway. You knew I wasn't feeling well. You knew I was terrified for Adrian. And yet—" She cocks her head, like she is somehow incredulous to my actions. Nothing I say will do any good. I know it won't. Whatever I say is pointless, so I don't say anything. I stand in the kitchen doorway, watching my dog throw a pine cone into the air and then chase it, his stumpy tail flapping away.

She throws her dishtowel onto the counter. "What am I supposed to do with you?"

My throat dries up. My heart pounds in my ears. My hands grow sticky with sweat. My knees rattle inside my pajamas.

"Don't just stand there. Talk to me!"

"I don't know, Mom."

I half expect for her to lunge at me, to take my shoulders and shake them till my head falls off. But she doesn't. She looks at me, disappointment dripping from every pore. "Well then, I don't either." She dries her hands on her nightgown and heads for the door.

"I did find Adrian," I squeak.

She turns and stares at me again, and again I freeze in my shoes. "And you don't think the detective would have?"

"No," I say, but it's such a little voice that I'm not sure even I hear it.

"Teddy. Darling. I know you meant well, but you have no idea what might have happened. I was worried sick about you, imagining you dead by the side of the road, shot by someone up in the hills or half-devoured by some bear. God only knows why the mind goes where it goes at times like these, but it does, and it was ugly. What if I had lost you too?"

"I know, Mom. I'm sorry."

"You should get dressed."

"Yes, Mom." I don't want to walk by her, so I linger at the back door as Arpeggio fills my heart with the joy of being home.

"Evvy's mother is lovely. Washing my dishes. Sitting at my table. Sipping tea with me. My God! She was terrified, too, and I didn't know what to do, and there was no note from you, no message, no phone call. Nothing! We thought you were dead."

"I know, Mom. I'm sorry."

"Sorry? That's all you can say? Sorry?"

I look at my feet. They're scraped and bruised. How did that happen?

"Well?"

I shake my head, and then I look at her. I try to look her in the eyes, but my focus keeps darting away. I take a deep breath. "No, Mom. I don't. I don't think the detective could do anything. You heard him. He said his hands were tied, that there was nothing he could do. That Dad is Adrian's legal dad, and so he has the right to travel with his son. But I had a feeling, Mom. In here." I touch my heart. "Adrian was in danger. Someone had to do something. So, if you want to beat me up or ground or throw me out of the house and swear you never want to see me again, go ahead. I did what I had to do. And I would do it again." I open the door, and Arpeggio bounds inside, sliding across the floor and landing squarely in front of his bowl. "You didn't see what I saw up there. What was happening to your son. I'm sorry, Mom, but Dad's not well, and I am not ready to see him."

She uncrosses her arms and opens to me for a hug. I am reluctant. I stop. I stall. I wait. But then that smile comes across her face, and I melt into her, and the tears come, and she holds me with her strong arms and tells me it's OK, and I choke on my tears and my breath and gulp for air.

We stand there, me squeezing into her soft body, until the tears subside and my breath comes back, and I pull away and look for a tissue. She hands me one from her pocket. Slightly used but perfect. So very perfect.

"OK. We'll talk to the hospital tomorrow."

CHAPTER 30

DAZED

"So glad to be home. How R U?"

I sleep most of the day, or if I'm awake, I'm in a daze. I think Evvy must be sleeping, too, because she doesn't answer her phone or her texts. Arpeggio sleeps in Adrian's lap, and the three of us sprawl across the couch, pretending to watch television, but most of the images fly by so fast I can't make sense of them, and the words fall into a haze. Still we sit there, while the big hand on the little clock marches around the dial and the sun peaks and sinks into the horizon. The room goes dark, and neither of us notices.

Until the light flicks on.

"I spoke with the doctor," Mom announces. "The hospital has agreed to keep your dad for forty-eight hours for observation." Mom steps in front of us and pulls the big wing-back chair in front of the TV. She crosses her legs and leans her elbow on her knee. I don't know why it all feels so rehearsed, but it does, like she's been practicing for the Uber ride home. "That's good news, isn't it?"

Adrian and I both mumble something like, "Yes, Mom."

She kicks off her shoes and rubs her feet, reminding us once again that she doesn't have a car anymore because it is still up on the hill, buried behind a large tree branch. "It wasn't easy," she says. "The doctors said he seems fine. The doctors said that he said that he and Adrian were on their way to school in the morning, just like the note said, and at the last minute, they decided to go to the cabin for a few days. On a lark. He said that they had forgotten their cell phones but that they were having such a nice time, and it was such a wonderful bonding time for them that, well, time got away from him. And I told them it wasn't what you kids had told me, but, well, you know these doctors. They said that what you said was so unbelievable that it was probably a dream."

"Did you really tell them?" I ask. "Did you tell them what we saw up there?"

"I tried, but now, well, now I don't know what to believe. Your father says he still wants to see you. Both of you. And your uncle Tony. Tony! Isn't that just the strangest thing you've ever heard of? All these years later, and who should show up but Tony! He always was a rascal." And she walks out of the room. "Lasagna?" she calls from the kitchen. "We also have some frozen corn."

"Sounds good," I call back.

"Now I know I'm home," Adrian says.

CHAPTER 31

PROSPERO'S LAST STAND

Six forty-two comes and goes with no morning memo from Evvy about what to wear to school. I text her to tell her that I'll be donning black leggings with heavy socks and my blue tunic sweater. The one that comes down to my knees. "It's cold today," I text. "Halloween's coming."

She isn't at the bus stop, and she isn't in the art room.

Lucky her, I think. *Her mom gave her the day off.*

"I trust you all had a restful weekend." Mr. Harrison closes the door and looks around the room, a big grin spreading across his face. His gaze rests on me; he looks me right in the eye. *What does he know?* My heart pounds against my ribs, and I flinch as the giant tree limb crashes around the car and once again, I am trapped.

"Well, okey dokey then." Mr. Harrison claps his hands, and his eyes shift to Tiger. She smiles back at him, and that's all he needs. "When we last left our heroes, they were following Caliban, getting quite drunk and bumbling their way across the island to Prospero's cabin. Do they know what they're looking for?"

"No," we say in unison.

"Excellent," says Mr. Harrison. He dons an invisible magic cloak and twirls his index finger into the air, a call for silence. "No. They do not know where they are going or what they are looking for. They are following Caliban, who has a plan, a scheme, an idea to murder Prospero and unleash himself from his evil master's iron grip. And lo and behold! They find the cabin! Right here! I mean—right here. With fresh clothes, fresh water, fresh food. Everything a man might want in a cabin."

He turns to the whiteboard and lifts his hands to God, and I'm back on the hill, up the gravel path, looking at the cabin for the first time: the red siding, the two windows, the door between them, the smoke in the chimney, the bench. He freezes, and the smoke freezes midair. He turns just his head, looking over his shoulder at us. "Natural or supernatural?"

No one says anything.

He unfreezes, and the cabin disappears. "Kim? What do you think?"

"I ... think Antonio and the clowns that are with him, well, they would probably see it all as magic, as supernatural. Where did it come from? Who lives here? But for us, in the audience, I think, well, we've met Prospero. We'd probably think it's natural."

"Very nice." Mr. Harrison pushes some papers aside and sits on his desk. His feet dangle.

"Yes. This is what we have been waiting for—the showdown between Prospero and Antonio. Prospero's revenge. What will he do with these poor slobs who think they lost their ship in a tempest, swam to shore, grieved the loss of each other, and now stand before him in his own clothes? Tiger? Any ideas?"

Tiger snaps her gum. She lifts her hands onto her desk and folds them, and if I didn't see her foot shaking beside me, I would say she had nothing but confidence in her bones. But she's really like the rest of us: scared of being seen as a fraud. She takes a deep breath and says, "Well, Mr. Harrison, I think if it were me, and my brother had put me out to sea with my four-year-old daughter on a leaky boat destined to sink, I'd want to see the look on his face when he sees me. Twelve years he's been waiting, reading his magic books and planning, scheming, and now it's here. And this dude—Antonio? He's so full of himself he probably doesn't even remember that he tried to murder his brother. Yeah. I'd say I want some revenge."

Mr. Harrison nods. "Anyone else?"

Kim's hand flaps like a flag on a schooner.

"Kim?"

"Can he turn them all into turtles and lizards with his magic?"

"He probably could," Mr. Harrison says. "If, of course, he could employ Ariel for one more task."

Everyone laughs, but they weren't at the table with five chairs; they weren't listening to my crazy-ass dad go off the deep end with his threats and his spells. They didn't hear the gun go off or teeter on the edge of the planet with nowhere to go but into the abyss with him. This guy—does Miranda think he's as scary as I do? She seems like she takes it all in stride. Like she's never known anything but his madness and his dreams of revenge. Every time she utters a concern, he like pats her on the head and says, "Now, now, little girl," and "It's just a storm. Just weather." And every time, she believes him!

"Edwina?"

I shake my head. He looks at me, and the room goes quiet. Everyone stares at me. I put my hands on my desk, just like Tiger did, and words come out. "What amazes me most is how Prospero can kidnap all these people, drag them to near death, threaten them with his magic spells, and everyone thinks he's this really cool guy. I mean, what he did—it was awful. Awfuller than awful. And ... and yet ..." I want to stop. I want to shut up, put a sock in it, but my mouth keeps going. "*The Tempest* is a romance. Happy ending. Does no one in this play have anything to say about that?"

Mr. Harrison looks at me for a full minute. What does he see? Does he know my dad? Finally, he speaks. "Wow," he says. Then "wow" again. "You are all so very right about Prospero. In his power, he is terrifying. He enslaved Ariel and Caliban and forced them to do his bidding. Ariel said, 'OK, I can fly and swim and move through fire,' but Caliban refused. He showed Prospero the magic of the island, and now he regrets ever helping him. He continued to despise his evil master. Prospero could twist the wind and manipulate men's journeys. But Edwina is right. *The Tempest* is not a tragedy. It is a romance. And as such, it is time for love to rise victorious. And though revenge is nigh, though it is in the palm of Prospero's hand, in this moment when he sees his brother and all his brother's friends, he stops. He takes off his magic cloak and lays it down. After twelve long years of plotting and planning, in this split second, he changes his mind. He gives up everything, and he forgives." Mr. Harrison sheds his own invisible cloak and folds it, laying it on the table the way a father would lay a new baby into a crib. "Happy ending." The room fills with a fairy-dust quiet, and joy ripples from desk to desk.

"Yes. Ferdinand has survived the log scene. He has risen to Prospero's impossible challenge, and now he can marry Miranda. So, come, come. Let us all gather around and celebrate this grand union of two sweet souls."

He walks across the room like a bride in the aisle, scattering imaginary flowers everywhere. He picks up Ariels' imaginary flute, and silent music fills the air. He picks up *The Tempest* and leans back.

> Now my charms are all o'erthrown
> And what strength I have's my own.

Mr. Harrison opens his eyes and says, "No matter how many times I read those lines, I am amazed. Yes. We are such stuff as dreams are made on, and now we must breathe deep and fill Prospero's sails, let him ride with his brother and the band of fools, back to his dukedom to live out his days as the rightful king. Antonio has been forgiven. Ariel is free. Caliban is free. And it is time for Prospero to give up everything—all his magic, all his regret, all his bitterness, and go. Leave the magical island of the stage."

> Now I want
> Spirits to enforce, art to enchant,
> And my ending is despair,
> Unless I be relieved by prayer,
> Which pierces so, that it assaults
> Mercy itself, and frees all faults.
> As you from crimes that would pardoned be
> Let your indulgence set me free.

I gaze out the window, and there is my dad, parading around the table with five chairs, his tattered red bathrobe hanging off his shoulders. Was that what he was going to do when Arpeggio flew out the door? Was he going to forgive his brother for the fire all those years ago? For driving him out of his little paradise in Las Vegas? Setting off his mental illness? Was he finally going to set me and Adrian free?

"In the end ..." Mr. Harrison paces the room, looking at his watch and pacing some more. "In the end, all we have is our own forgiveness, our own spirit of love. 'Forgiveness does not change the past, but it does enlarge the future.'" He laughs. "That's from my fortune cookie. Not Shakespeare. But I hope in our time together, I have taught you something about finding wisdom in even the oddest places. So, let us all clap and set old Prospero free. Let him take the last of his wind and sail safely back to Milan." And just like that, everyone takes a deep breath. One breath. From all of us. And we clap. And Mr. Harrison bows, and Prospero evaporates into the thin air of the whiteboard.

The room is quiet for the longest time. A comfortable quiet. The quiet of endurance and accomplishment. Finally, Mr. Harrison stands up and says, "Yes. I will miss Mr. Shakespeare. He has been a fine companion for all my years of teaching. But I believe I hear my husband at the door, and if that is true, then my prayers have been answered. It is time now for me to welcome this new chapter of my life."

He opens the door, and in walks a tall, lean, handsome man with black hair, black-rimmed eyeglasses, and a smile that could melt snow. "This, my friends, is my husband, Ben Silverman." He nods to us, but he only has eyes for a small bundle that he hands off to Mr. Harrison.

The bundle begins to cry.

We all clap and cry and whistle and stamp our feet and cry some more as this tiny little thing—maybe two months old? All swabbed in pink with a little ribbon on her head and beautiful tawny brown skin—is passed around, and we each count her fingers and count her toes and touch her lips and kiss her forehead and pass her on.

"But, Mr. Harrison," Kim says, "does that mean you're leaving?
A deathly pall falls over the room.

"Yes. Your Mr. Harrison will, from this time forward, be known as Dad. Ms. Sarah Smith from Albany High has offered to finish the semester for me. But do not despair. I will still direct the play this fall, and auditions are coming up on Friday, so get your speeches ready."

And then the bell rings. As if it were any other Monday. I linger at the door, hoping he will call me back, ask me to stay, to hold this new bundle of tears and joy. But he doesn't. And silently we file out into the noisy hallway.

CHAPTER 32

UNDER THE GUILDER TREE

"Meet us at the river," I text

Adrian, Arpeggio, and I bundle up in hats and scarves and trudge through the chilly woods behind our house to the river. The trail fills with soft yellow leaves, and patches of snow linger with the dying ferns. None of us says much of anything, but we all feel very close. I look at my feet, and with each step they take, I rediscover that I am still alive. Was it a dream? Was I in Kansas all along? Or will I wake up and find myself back in the cabin with Dad still raging against the wind? I don't know where Teddy leaves off and my dad begins. Where reality—what I can hear and see with my senses—ends and my dreams begin. It's all a blur.

But my feet keep walking up the hill, and the trees keep singing with the winds in their leaves. This path is so familiar now. I know its shadows and its dappled sunlight, its tree roots and its stones. Adrian and I walk in silence until we come to the river. The trees part, and the sky opens. October blue, with soft white clouds floating in the breeze. I look for Evvy, but she isn't here.

Adrian grins. "We made it, Teddy."

"We did," I say, and then something fills the silence. It's nothing tangible, nothing I could even describe, but it's there, a tenderness, an aging, a journey that Adrian and Arpeggio and I have been on. I am Adrian's hero. For one brief moment, I did something. I was part of a rescue for my brother. Nothing in our lives will ever change that. I was more scared and more brave than I ever thought I could be, and now we're back here, on this sandy, grassy patch of beach along the banks of the river.

"Evvy should be here," he says.

"I know," I say. "I think she's tired."

Adrian nods. "What do you think will happen to Dad?"

"I don't know." I bend down and pick up a stone. It's about the size of a half dollar and flat. "Hold out your hand," I say, and he does. I lay the stone in the palm of his hand. "It's time to make a wish."

He squeezes his eyes shut and turns the stone over and over in his hands until it is warm. "Yes," he says. "We need a ritual today. A way to say that we have grown up. Not all the way, maybe, but a little bit. That we have met the dragon, and we have lived." He grins. "So, now you find a stone for you."

I find a stone, all black with a white stripe running all the way around. *A lucky stone*, I think, for Arpeggio, who rescued us all. We take off our shoes and put our feet in the cold sand. I pick up a stick for Arpeggio, and on the count of three, Adrian and I close our eyes and hurl our stones far out into the water. They land with a plunk and drift into the deepest belly of the river. And there they settle, his stone and my stone, side by side, on the bottom of the river bed, reunited with the People of the Waters That Are Never Still.

"Good," Adrian says. "And now, if we ever have doubts about ourselves or what we can do, we can come back to this spot and remember these stones."

We wrap our arms around each other, and I throw the stick for Arpeggio. He leaps into the cold water and swims for it. When he steps back onto the shore, he gives a good shake, spraying water on both me and Adrian.

The afternoon sun settles on the tops of the trees. Our shadows grow long and skinny. I hold Adrian close and take out my phone, snapping a picture of this moment. Arpeggio wriggles into the shadow. A falcon cries, soaring overhead.

We step gingerly onto the dim light of the trail.

"Do you think Evvy's OK?" he asks. "I mean, do you think she's freaked out about Dad?"

My heart skips a beat. "No," I say. "Evvy's different from the others. She kissed me under the Guilder Tree, and that means our love will last forever."

"Are you talking about the chestnut tree at the end of the trail?"

"Exactly. Seems there was a horrible feud in Crystal Falls. There were two families, hated each other. No one knows why. Anyway, it was way back in the 1700s, I think. And one night in some kind of shootout, a little boy was caught in the crossfire and killed. By accident. So, the families, in their grief, planted that tree and promised that the tree would bring eternal love to the town. So, it turns out that if you ever kiss someone under the Guilder Tree, your love will last forever."

"That's nice."

"I kissed Evvy there. Last summer."

"So that means you guys are going to be OK?"

"Exactly."

Adrian stops. "Teddy? Someone's on the trail. Up ahead."

I squint my eyes to see. "OMG! Adrian! Arpeggio! Come on. It's Evvy! She's at the tree. She's waiting for us. Evvy!" Arpeggio leaps into the air and takes off in a run. Adrian and I are right behind.

"Arpeggio!" she squeals, and the dog dives into her arms, spilling her sketch pad onto the ground along with her pencils and charcoal and erasers. I bend down to pick them up. Adrian gives her a big hug, and she hugs him back, and tears form in her eyes.

I am just about to hug her also, but I stop. "I've been trying to call and text and stuff." I pant, trying to catch my breath.

"I know," she says, taking her pencils.

I get down on one knee and help her pick things up. "How are you?"

She shakes her head. "Not very well." She stands, stuffing everything into her bag. "I'm sorry," she says. "I have to go."

"Wait," I say, and she waits.

She shifts her weight from one foot to another. "What?"

"Are ... you mad at me?"

"Oh, gee, Teddy. I can't think why. You lure me into your mother's car and send me on a wild goose chase. Damned near get me killed. I have to deal with your father for two days. Yes! And ..."

"And?" I ask.

"No." She looks away. "It's my mom. She says I can't see you anymore. She says she liked you, but your family is crazy, clinically crazy, and she doesn't think you're good for me. I'm sorry, Teddy. It's what it is."

She starts to go, but I grab her by the arm. Her sketch pad falls to the ground and opens onto a page: a cabin, faded red, on a hill, with two windows and a door between, a chimney with smoke rising.

"That's the cabin," I say.

"It's Prospero's cabin now." Tears are running down her cheeks. She picks up the sketch pad and crosses her arms over it, but I take it anyway. She doesn't stop me.

"And down here, that's the tree that fell on the car. It's the log scene." I look at her, and she nods, so I turn the page. There is my dad in his red bathrobe with his seven-day old beard. "Is that Prospero?" I ask, and she nods and turns the page. A man in a perfectly pressed three-piece linen suit and felt hat stands in the middle of the page.

"Uncle Tony?" I ask. And she nods.

"Yeah. Antonio. There's one more," she says. "But you might not want to see it."

"Is it me?"

"No." She turns the page. A boy, maybe twelve years old, sits huddled on a cot in the corner of the cabin. He's terrified of something. His back has the shell of a tortoise.

"Caliban?" I ask, and she nods.

"I'm sorry, Teddy. I know they're your family, but I can't see anything else. I close my eyes, and I'm haunted. I can't practice the piano. I can't read. I can't draw anything but this. I'm supposed to come up with all this stuff for Mr. Harrison before auditions on Friday, but none of it matters. What happened out there—I was so scared, but, Teddy, you were so brave. We were out there, on the edge of someplace I have never been. I've been trying to talk to my mom, but she won't listen. I dream about it, and no matter where I start the dream—sometimes it starts in school, sometimes in a canoe on the river—every time, I end up in an eddy of water, spinning in circles, and then we're at the cabin."

I don't say anything. I sit and listen to her, and I know we share more than just this one dream. My heart breaks in a thousand pieces as she tells me she's afraid of me, afraid I will be just like my dad. She could see it. Up there. At the cabin. The ways in which I lose my grip on reality. "And my mom. She tells me I have to think of myself sometimes, have to take care of … I … I think it's better this way."

"But … but … no, Evvy. Please. You can't."

"I know. I kissed you under the Guilder Tree and promised that I would love you forever. And I will love you. Nothing can ever change that. But I'm sorry. I can't."

The moon rises in the sky, just over there, between those trees. The leaves have all fallen, and the bare branches reveal everything.

"I really am sorry," she says.

And then she turns and walks away.

CHAPTER 33

ENOUGH IS ENOUGH

"She's gone?" Adrian asks.

"Yup. Just like everyone else who has ever met my family. I really thought she was different."

We walk home in silence, but it's not the silence of two souls touching; it's the silence of two bubbles, each one filled with sorrow.

"The detective went up to the cabin," Mom says when we step in the door. "He and the sergeant restocked the food and the beer and the firewood and the clothes. They even replaced the vodka. And he got my car back. It has a few scratches, but it's fine. Runs like a charm."

"That's nice," I say, but I don't care.

And then she drops the big one. "I made arrangements for you to see your father tomorrow after school, so come right home, you hear me?"

"Perfect," I say. "Just when I thought this day couldn't get any worse." I pour Arpeggio's kibble into his bowl and climb the endless

staircase to my bedroom, where I manage to close the door before I
burst into tears.

Everything after that is a blur. That night. School the next day.
Meeting the new English teacher. Lunch. Kim says something to me
about the audition, but I don't care. I am wrapped in gauze.

I get on the bus to come home. Evvy does not get on with me.
She is up ahead on the street. Her shoulders are slumped, and she's
dragging herself along. I want to call to her. More than anything on
this whole planet, I want to talk with her one more time, to say how
sorry I am about the car and my dad and dragging her into it and what
a fool I was. I knew it would happen. I knew if she spent time with
my family, she would run. But I did it anyway, and over and over, I
spin that morning when I snuck into Mom's purse and took the keys.
And every time, I get on the bus like I'm supposed to and go to school
like I'm supposed to, and every time when I get home, Adrian and
Dad are there, and they're fine, and let's have lasagna.

But that's not what happened.

I sit by the window, squeezed next to some boy who smells like
burnt marshmallows.

"I have to get my dog."

Mom and Adrian are in the car when I get home.

"He can't come," Mom says.

"Then I can't come."

"Teddy? Please." She sighs.

I take Arpeggio to a tree near out house. "Quick pee," I tell him,
and he understands. At least he understands me. I think I will give
up on friends and just have a dog. He doesn't ask my family to be
normal. He only wants to be loved. That's enough. I kiss him goodbye,

so unsure if I will see him later or if I will once again be swallowed whole by my dad.

In silence, we drive the long, winding streets to the hospital. It's the same road we took to Warren's Dairy, only this time Mom takes a turn to the left and then down a long road with a stone wall on one side and a barbed wire fence on the other. Maple trees overhang the road. They have gone bright red now.

The front desk staff say hi to Mom like they know her, like she's been here every day, like they're all old friends. "He's waiting for you in the cafeteria," she says. "You know where it is?"

Mom nods and leads us forward.

The cafeteria is exactly what I thought it would be: a room with eight oblong, folding tables, each one with six chairs, everything nailed to the floor. Sunlight filters in through greasy windows. Small windows, up at the top of the wall. Pink concrete walls. Black linoleum floor. How is anyone supposed to get better in a place like this?

Uncle Tony is at a table in the corner with Dad. There is an open Bible between them. They hold hands. Uncle Tony is reading a passage, and Dad is listening, his eyes closed. He's still wearing that stupid bathrobe. We slide into chairs and sit.

"Tony?" my mom says.

"Hello, Harriet." He stands and gives her a hug and a kiss on her cheek. "How are you?"

"I'm fine." She pulls away and sits as far from Dad as she can, leaving me and Adrian squeezed in between her and him.

"Yes. Well, it seems like I was part of Sullivan's master plan."

"Sullivan? Can you tell me what really happened up in that cabin?"

"Shh, Harriet. Sullivan says it's time to listen now."

I am ready to race Adrian to the door, swing out of the cafeteria, back down the hall and out the front, to the fresh air and manicured garden and into the mountains. I do not want to sit in this awful chair. Not for an hour. Not for a minute. Prospero forgave his brother, and everyone lived happily ever after, but I can't do that. I've had enough of my dad's requests and commands to last me a lifetime. I fold my arms over my chest, throw one leg over the other knee, and kick the air.

"Teddy?" Dad slurs my name.

"What?"

"I want you to hear this."

"Fine. Talk."

"He's still on a lot of meds," Uncle Tony says. "Thorazine. Just till he really calms down. It's hard for him to talk. You have to really listen."

"I know I've been ..." Dad says, but then he stops and looks around. He sees us, and tears form in the corner of his eyes.

"Wait, Sully. It's OK. Let me start." Tony puts his elbows on the table and props himself up. "I came here this morning because I had to tell your dad"—he turns to us, swallowing and taking a breath—"that I am truly, deeply sorry. I have been carrying this guilt and shame inside me for so long now I didn't even know it was still there. I told myself that Las Vegas wasn't that awful for your dad. He got a pretty penny from the insurance, and I convinced myself I did right by him. Every last cent went for your dad. But somewhere I knew. Of course I knew. I could just never admit it. I thought the fire was a lark, a stupid, horrible way for me to hold onto my life, and that once I got out of prison, I could finally be free. But of course, I wasn't. I'm not." He turns to my dad. "When I saw you up you there at the cabin, in that beard and your bathrobe, well, even then I couldn't admit it. But I see it now, and I'm sorry, Sully. I truly am."

Dad nods his head and mumbles something like a thank you. He smiles and tries to stand, but he teeters. Uncle Tony grabs him and shimmies around the table to hold him up. Dad holds onto the chair with one hand and takes the robe off with other. He folds it neatly, lays it on the table, and sits again.

"Teddy?" he slurs, and a tear forms in the corner of his eye. His nose drips, and it takes everything I have not to leap up and wipe it for him. But Tony puts his hand on Dad's arm. "Go on, Sully."

"Teddy. Adrian. I was telling your uncle earlier, before the Thorazine kicked in, that I also owe you both an apology. More than an apology. I owe you your childhood. Not because I'm crazy. I can't help that." Dad nods and laughs, a tiny breath of air escaping from his lips. "But for not getting help. For not taking the help I was given seriously. Or graciously."

He rolls his eyes, and his words all slur. He might as well be speaking in Russian, but I catch some of it. "Adrian ... ashamed ... my son ... a baseball ... after dinner ... but you ... blind ... and, and, and I punished you."

"It's all right, Sullivan," Mom says. "You don't have to speak. If it's too hard—"

"No!" Dad slaps the table. It's a weak, flaccid slap, but the tear in his eye rolls down his cheek. He wipes it off with his sleeve. We all sit back. "And, Teddy, I wanted you to be pretty and demure ... a ponytail with yellow ribbons. But you're queer. Oh, don't try to deny it. I know you are. I've known it for years. Probably long before you did. But you're making a life for yourself. A good one, from the looks of it. My life has been my own doing. Not the disease. The disease I inherited. But my life. The one that I have wasted on anger and the lust for revenge? That one is all mine."

He licks his lips, dry from the medication he is on, and Tony lifts a plastic cup. Dad takes a sip. He wipes his lips with a stiff paper napkin.

"Shall I?" Tony asks, and Dad nods.

"The doctor says it's bipolar disorder. Our grandfather had it too, although they didn't call it that at the time, and they didn't have any meds for it. She knows a place near Buffalo, New York, that she says is very good. She says they can help him stabilize on the meds. But he'll be gone a long time. Two months. Maybe three. Do you think you can do that, Sull?"

Dad nods. "I ... go. Harriet? Will you ..."

Mom walks around the table and sits next to Dad. She takes his hand. "I would like you to get some help," she says.

"Thank you," he says.

Adrian puts his hand on Dad's arm. "I'm sorry I tried to shoot you."

"No, you're not." Dad laughs. And then we all laugh. Dad has given up everything. Like Prospero, he's given up his magic, his resentment, his rage. He sits before us, a man humbled by life's power.

"Teddy?" Tony says.

I look at him. I just lost the love of my life because of him, and I'm supposed to say, "Yeah, go for it, Dad. Everything's fine, Dad"? It's a stretch and not one I'm sure I want to make. For so much of my life, friends have come and gone like the water in the river, while Adrian and I have drowned like our two stones. But I look around the table. This is my family. They're here to stay. Love them or hate them, they're mine. They're in my blood. I reach out and put my hand on theirs. Tony wraps both of his around ours, and together we shake.

CHAPTER 34

THE LAST LOG SCENE

On Friday morning, at 6:42, I check my phone. Still no news from Evvy. No morning wardrobe report. No "I'm so sorry I can't live without you please forgive me." Mom is up, making toast and coffee. She goes back to work today.

"Come home right after school. You hear me?"

"I'm going to audition for the play."

"You can't do that."

"Yes, I can."

"I forbid it."

"I don't care." I grab Arpeggio's leash and put my hand on the doorknob.

"But what about Adrian? Who's going to be here when he gets home? Teddy, we have to—"

I turn to her and put my hand up. That stops her. I smile because, just like they are my family, I am theirs. Whatever happens, I am here to stay. "He and I talked last night. He's taking the bus to the high school. If I get in, he'll come when I have rehearsal. He'll hang around. Maybe he'll even get to work on the play somehow. But we will catch the late bus and come home together. Arpeggio knows too. He'll be fine."

"The late bus? But what if you miss it? You can't just call me, you know."

"Then—" I want to choke on my words, but I don't. I look her straight in the eye and go on. "Then Kim, a girl in my English class, can give us a ride home. Her mom just got an SUV. Plenty of room. It'll be fine. You can't stop me, Mom. Not anymore."

"Oh." She looks at me.

And I look at her.

I am in my body. I am alive.

The hallway in front of Mr. Harrison's classroom is buzzing with kids.

"Did you sign in?" Kim asks me.

"Not yet."

"It's over here," she says, and she shows me the table with the pages with sixteen kids signed in ahead of me. Five of them are trying out for Ariel. "What number are we on now?" I ask.

"I think this is number nine. So, only seven to go. My best guess is about"—she looks at her phone—"forty minutes."

I find two chairs across the hall, and I sit. Tiger comes and sits with me. "Who are you trying out for?" she asks.

"Ariel. How about you?"

"Prospero," she says. "I have an old grudge I need to let go of." She looks at me and laughs. "Not you, Teddy. Oh no. You're fine." She touches my arm. "My dad. He left when I was seven. Just like that. I've always hated him for that. Maybe if I play Prospero, I can find a way to forgive."

"There is something in this play," I say. "Some kind of magic."

"Teddy?" Adrian shows up. He's wandering down the hall, banging into lockers and doorjambs. "Teddy?"

"Over here, Adrian." I leap up and take him by his arm. "It's going to be a wait, I'm afraid. There are a million kids ahead of me."

"That's OK," he says.

"I'm Tiger. Teddy's friend from English."

Wow. She called me her friend.

"Adrian," he says. He points his hand in her general direction, and she takes it in both of hers, squeezing it with such respect.

"How was school?" I ask.

But his answer doesn't matter. Nothing matters anymore except that Evvy has left me, Tiger is my new friend, and Adrian is here. The minutes tick by, and the hall thins out. And then it's my turn.

"Teddy?" It's Evvy. At the door. Calling my name.

I start to leave. "No. I can't do this. It's too much. You never told me—"

"No, Teddy, please. Come in. It's your turn."

"Break a leg," Tiger says.

"Thanks."

Adrian and I step into the room.

"Hello, Edwina," Mr. Harrison says. "How are you today?"

My knees are shaking. My mouth is dry. My hands are dripping with sweat. The desks have been pushed up against the walls, leaving an open space in the middle of the room. "I'm fine," I say. "This is my brother, Adrian. Adrian, this is my English teacher, Mr. Harrison."

"Hi," Adrian says.

"It's very nice to meet you. I was wondering"—Mr. Harrison looks at Evvy and smiles—"if we could try something a little different here today. So, Edwina, if you could turn to act three, scene one. And, Evermore, if you could begin on line ..." He skims through the scene. "What did you say, Evermore?"

"Line seventy-four."

"Sir?" I say.

"You heard me."

"But, sir. This is—"

Evvy comes to the center of the room with me. "It was my idea," she says.

"What? You're auditioning now? I thought you said ..."

"I said a lot of horrible things. Please, Teddy. With me on this?"

My head is spinning, and I think I'm going to either faint or throw up. But there's Mr. Harrison's voice: "OK then. Let's take it from the top. Edwina, you are Ferdinand. You are moving the logs. Miranda, you enter and see him working. Edwina. You begin."

Once again, I am asked to do the impossible. I stumble into the text.

> The very instant that I saw you, did
> My heart fly to your service, there resides
> To make me slave to it, and for your sake,
> Am I this patient log-man.

And Evvy stands before me: Miranda, and before my very eyes, she slips into the skin of this fair maiden and asks, "Do you love me?"

My knees quake beneath me, and I read:

Oh heaven! Oh earth! Bear witness to this sound,
And crown what I profess with kind event
If I speak true. I
Do love, prize, honor you.

Evvy's eyes glisten in the afternoon light.

I am a fool
To weep at what I am glad of.

And then she takes me in her arms and holds me and whispers in my ear, "Teddy Carson. I want this life with you. However long it lasts, whatever it may bring, 'if you tell me first that you love me, then I will tell you, I love you, too.'"

"I love you," I say.

And then the lights fade to black.

SPECIAL THANKS

This book is not my story. I was never kidnapped. I never had to go on a hero's quest to find my brother. But it is my truth. Growing up in a family with mental illness and blindness has given me a relationship with the netherworld, the space between the real and the unreal. This space is in all my writing. I do not have answers for it, but like Psyche and Persephone, I am driven by an insatiable curiosity to unveil its language.

There are many people instrumental in the development of this book, and, frankly, without them, it would still be a pile of ribbons on my kitchen floor:

First is Donita Hill, my reader who has been through so many drafts of so many books and who always guides my characters toward love. Tatiana Messina-Schwartz has offered me a friendship that has spanned nearly thirty years. I am indebted to her insistence for truth and her reminders that there is nothing more important than love.

Ros Thomas-Clark has an enduring love of theatre and Shakespeare. "Write about *The Tempest*," she said. "Prospero gives up everything." Her granddaughter, Bronwyn Clark, twelve years old, had so much to say about these characters and this story, I was overwhelmed and inspired. Likewise, my dear friend Azize Salamé, who reads, who draws, who paints, who hums, who always has a song in her heart, tore through this book in a day and a half and came up breathless. Seth Hill offered an amazing vulnerability and honesty to the process. His experiences followed me everywhere. Rhoda Grill brought such a broad understanding of mental health and survival in an impossible world. She also has a love of Shakespeare and "characters who behave badly." Sarah Kingsbury, who I have known since I was nine days old, always brings me back to the inspiration and the healing power of nature.

I owe a deep understanding of Shakespeare to the casts of so many plays at the youth wing of Actors Shakespeare Company. When I asked them who, in *The Tempest* was truly capable of love, they gave me the play in all its glory and hardship.

Judith Lindquist is simply the best damn writing teacher I've ever met. Mark Spencer read and read again and brought such joy and energy to Mr. Harrison. He gave fabulous line notes and questions about what the hell I was doing.

Gabe Thornton offered his love of the law and his work for social justice.

Marianne Verhaegen gave me the last piece of courage I needed to send this off.

And Jane Myers helped me steady my canoe in a rising storm. She wasn't always successful, but she always tried. I don't think we can ask more than that.

Printed in the United States
by Baker & Taylor Publisher Services